BY RENÉE WATSON

RENÉE WATSON

illustrated by Nina Mata

BLOOMSBURY
CHILDREN'S BOOKS
NEW YORK LONDON OXFORD NEW DELHI SYDNEY

BLOOMSBURY CHILDREN'S BOOKS
Bloomsbury Publishing Inc., part of Bloomsbury Publishing Plc
1385 Broadway, New York, NY 10018

BLOOMSBURY, BLOOMSBURY CHILDREN'S BOOKS, and the Diana logo
are trademarks of Bloomsbury Publishing Plc

First published in the United States of America in April 2020
by Bloomsbury Children's Books

Text copyright © 2020 by Renée Watson
Interior art © 2020 by Nina Mata

Bloomsbury books may be purchased for business or promotional use. For
information on bulk purchases please contact Macmillan Corporate and
Premium Sales Department at specialmarkets@macmillan.com

Library of Congress Cataloging-in-Publication Data
Names: Watson, Renée, author.
Title: Ways to make sunshine / by Renée Watson.
Description: [New York] : Bloomsbury Children's Books, 2020.
Summary: The Hart family of Portland, Oregon, faces many setbacks after Ryan's
father loses his job, but no matter what, Ryan tries to bring sunshine to her loved ones.
Identifiers: LCCN 2019046159 (print) ● LCCN 2019046160 (e-book)
ISBN 978-1-5476-0056-4 (hardcover) ● ISBN 978-1-5476-0057-1 (e-book)
Subjects: CYAC: Family life—Oregon—Portland—Fiction. | Schools—Fiction. |
African Americans—Fiction. | Portland (Or.)—Fiction.
Classification: LCC PZ7.1.S47 Way 2020 (print) | LCC PZ7.1.S47 (e-book) |
DDC [Fic]—dc23
LC record available at https://lccn.loc.gov/2019046159
LC e-book record available at https://lccn.loc.gov/2019046160

ISBN 978-1-5476-0579-8 (exclusive edition)

Book design by Danielle Ceccolini
Typeset by Westchester Publishing Services
Printed and bound in the U.S.A. by Berryville Graphics Inc., Berryville, Virginia
4 6 8 10 9 7 5

To find out more about our authors and books visit www.bloomsbury.com and sign up
for our newsletters.

For my goddaughter, Ryan Hart.
You are my sunshine.

CONTENTS

THE GIRL WHO COULD BE KING

I AM A GIRL with a name that a lot of boys have. So when the substitute teacher takes roll and calls out, "Ryan?" she looks surprised when I answer. I wish Ms. Colby were here. Ms. Colby doesn't even need to take roll anymore because it is the first day of March and she's been teaching us for six months, so she can tell who is here and who is not just by looking across the room. Ms. Colby always starts the day off with our Thumbs-Up/Thumbs-Down/Somewhere-in-the-Middle Check-In. This substitute teacher doesn't do any of that and so I don't get to show my thumbs-up for making perfect scrambled eggs and toast this morning.

I wonder why Ms. Colby didn't leave a note for the sub with a list of do's and don'ts. Like *don't* call DeVonté, DeVonté—call him D. And *don't* look so shocked when a girl raises her hand when you call out for Ryan.

"Here," I say.

"Ryan Hart?" the substitute says. She looks at me like she is not sure I am who I say I am.

"Yes. My name is Ryan."

"Oh," she says, pushing up her too-big glasses.

Brandon, the boy sitting next to me, says, "She has a boy's name."

I roll my eyes at him because no one is talking to him and he needs to mind his own business. "I do not have a boy's name. I have *my* name. My name is Ryan and Ryan means 'king' and that means I am a leader—"

"Okay, ah, please settle down. Settle down," the substitute teacher says, mostly to me and not to Brandon, who thinks he knows it all. "Okay, Ryan Hart is here," she says to herself.

Then Brandon whispers, "And she spells her last name wrong." He laughs at his corny joke.

"I do not! My name is Ryan Hart and it's not heart like the muscle, it's H-A-R-T as in . . . as in *my* last name."

The substitute teacher walks over to my desk and says, "I need you to keep your voice down."

"I need Brandon to leave me alone!" I roll my eyes at Brandon again, extra roll this time, but then I remember what Mom always tells me, how she named me Ryan because she wanted me to feel powerful, to remember that I am a leader every time someone calls my name. Dad is always telling me our people come from royalty, that my ancestors lived in Africa and were kings and queens and inventors and hard workers. Mom tells me their strength is running through my veins.

I sit up straight, ignore Brandon, and try to be the leader I am supposed to be.

Mom and Dad tell me I will keep growing into my name. They say it to my brother, too. "Be who we named you to be," they tell him whenever he is pulling my ponytail or grabbing food off my plate when I'm not looking.

My brother's name is Raymond. We call him Ray. His name means "protector" and Dad says he should be keeping me, his little sister, safe. But mostly he is just bossy and nosy and sometimes he treats me like I am a glass thing that could break. He is always telling me *you can't do this* and *you shouldn't be so that.* Maybe because I am two years younger than him, maybe because I am a girl. Maybe because he doesn't know the meaning of my name, how tough I really am.

Maybe he doesn't realize I can do and be anything.

When it's time to go outside for recess, Brandon, Marcus, and the boy with glasses who I never talk to are splashing around in the puddles and stomping in mud. Then they race each other up the monkey bars. I walk over to join in on the climbing but before I can get there, the substitute teacher says to me, "Why don't you go over there, sweetheart?" and points to the swings and slide.

I'd rather stay here, pretending to climb a mountain, so I say, "No, thank you," and keep walking to the monkey bars. The substitute teacher follows me and that's when I realize that it wasn't a suggestion or question. It was a demand.

"I really think it'll be safer if you stay off the monkey bars. Besides, you and Brandon might need a break from each other."

"I'll stay out of Brandon's way," I say. "And I don't think it's dangerous. I play on them all the time. I bet I can even climb faster than those boys."

Just then, Brandon shouts out, "You can't beat me!" and he jumps down—showing off. "I bet you a pack of green apple Jolly Ranchers that you can't beat me. Let's race."

"Race?"

"Yeah, last one to that pole has to buy the winner

candy." He points to the tetherball pole across the playground.

I think about it. There's a small crowd forming and now I feel like I have to say yes, like I have to prove to the substitute teacher that I can play whatever I want, with whoever I want. "I don't like Jolly Ranchers," I tell Brandon. "When I win, you have to buy me a Twix."

I look over at KiKi, one of my best friends. She smiles and gives us our countdown. "On your mark . . . Get set . . . Go!"

I hear our friends all cheering but mostly I hear the sound of my breath huffing and puffing, in and out, in and out. My feet slap the pavement and I run as fast as I can. Brandon is beating me but not by much. I move my arms through the air, forcing myself to go faster. I catch up and then, just like I knew I could, I start running faster than Brandon. By a lot. I am winning. I am winning!

The pole is close and if I stretch my arm out far enough, I'll reach it. I run a few more steps and then, when I go to put my right foot down, something happens. My right foot doesn't touch the pavement the way a running foot usually touches the pavement. Instead, it stumbles and hiccups its way to the cold ground.

I have fallen. Blood is trickling out of my knee and there's a stinging and pounding feeling all through my leg.

Instead of stopping the race and seeing if I am okay, Brandon runs right past me, tags the pole, and says, "Yes! Beat you. You owe me a pack of Jolly Ranchers."

"No fair," KiKi yells. "She was at the pole first. It's not her fault her shoe was untied."

I didn't even realize that's what happened. My shoe is untied. I tripped over my shoelace.

"Don't be a sore loser," Brandon says.

"He's right," I tell KiKi. "I never touched the pole."

Dad picks us up from school and the first thing he asks me is, "What happened to your jeans?" He looks at the hole, then back at me. "It's a long story," I tell him. He doesn't press me but I'm sure Mom will.

On the way home, I ask if we can stop at the corner store. When Dad says yes, I ask Ray, "Do you have two dollars?"

He answers, "Why?" and this means he has two dollars, he's just not sure if he wants to give them to me.

I hold my hand out. "I'll pay you back."

He gives me two dollars and when we get to the corner store, I go straight to the candy aisle and buy a pack of green apple Jolly Ranchers for Brandon. And a Twix for me.

The Thing About Ice Cream

WHEN RAY AND I get home, I go straight to my room to change my jeans before Mom asks any questions. When I come back downstairs, Dad and Mom are setting out bowls and spoons on the dining room table. "Hope you had a great day at school," Mom says. "We thought we'd have a little treat," she tells us.

Dad brings two pints of ice cream out of the freezer and asks, "Which flavor should I open?"

Usually Mom and Dad only let us have ice cream for dessert but never, ever before dinner. I know something is up.

I am sitting across from Ray at the dining room table. I look at Ray, a little surprised, a little worried. "What's wrong, Dad?" Ray asks.

"Nothing's wrong," Dad says. "Which flavor?"

Ray only likes plain things (like steamed broccoli with no melted cheese and cheese pizza with no pepperoni, or mushrooms, or crunchy bell peppers). He doesn't have adventurous taste buds like I do, so of course he picks vanilla.

I like vanilla and chocolate and strawberry. I like dulce de leche and peppermint and cookies and cream. But most of all I love Tillamook's Marionberry Pie ice cream. The rich vanilla ice cream is mixed with fresh Oregon marionberries and big chunks of piecrust. I always eat it slow so it can last and last.

Why are we breaking our no-dessert-before-dinner rule?

"Chocolate, please," I say.

Ray shouts out "Family vote!" because he knows that Dad likes vanilla better than chocolate.

It's a tie—Dad and Ray for vanilla, Mom and me for chocolate. We usually settle ties with a round of rock-paper-scissors but instead I tell them, "It doesn't matter. Vanilla is fine."

Mom holds her hand out toward Dad to stop him from opening the pint of vanilla ice cream. "Are you sure, Ryan?"

"Vanilla is fine," I repeat. I mean, it's not that I don't like vanilla. It's just not my favorite. And really, I just want to get to the reason why we're breaking our no-dessert-before-dinner rule.

Dad scoops out ice cream for each of us and then it happens. Mom says, "So we wanted to have a little treat to celebrate some good news." She looks at Dad, passing the announcement on to him like she's tagging him in a game of chase.

"We are going to be moving to a new house," Dad says.

Then Mom adds, "We found a nice place that's not too far from here."

My bowl of ice cream sits in front of me. I haven't taken one bite.

Ray is eating his, but slowly now. Most of the time, Ray's ice cream barely starts to melt, he gobbles it so fast. "Why are we moving?" he asks.

"The landlord is selling this house, so we needed to find another place to live."

I ask Mom, "But why is he selling the house when he already has us living here?"

Mom touches my hand. "It's his house, sweetheart. He can sell it whenever he wants to."

"Why don't you just buy it from him since he's selling it? Can't he sell it to us?" I ask.

Ray says, "Ryan, we can't afford to buy a house. Dad isn't working anymore. Stop asking so many questions. They told us things might change."

"But Dad is going to get a new job, isn't he?" Dad worked at the post office for fifteen years. Six months ago, his post office closed and he's been out of work ever since.

"Well, actually," Dad says, "I do have a new job. Which is another reason why we're celebrating. It's just that this new job pays less than my old job—"

"A lot less," Mom says.

"So we have to make some adjustments," Dad tells us.

This is nothing to celebrate.

I am trying really hard not to cry but I can't help it. I must look so pitiful sitting here in front of melting vanilla ice cream with tears streaming down my face. Ray doesn't even call me a crybaby, so I know I must look extra pitiful. Mom squeezes my hand. "It's okay to be sad. Change is scary."

Dad tries to make me feel better. "I think you'll like our new home, Ryan. You both will have your own rooms."

That's a good thing, I guess. I would love to have my own space and not just one side of a room. But still. This is the only house I've ever lived in. I don't want to leave. "Will we still go to the same school?" I ask.

"Yes, you will still go to Vernon but instead of Dad dropping you off in the morning you two will be able to walk together."

"Walk?" Ray asks.

"Yes, your mom and I are selling the second car, and now that we're moving closer to your school, you two can walk. It's only three blocks away," Dad says. "I'll be working the midnight shift, so I won't be home in the morning anymore when you leave for school."

I really like Dad driving us to school, how he lets us pick the song we want to hear and how we sing loud the whole ride, how he kisses both of us on the forehead—even Ray—before we go inside, how he tells us "Be who we named you to be" as we get out of the car.

Who will ask "Got your homework?" before I walk out of the house and who will I wave goodbye to when I get to the school door?

Mom looks at me and says, "We'll be living closer to KiKi. I've already talked with her mom, and you three will walk to school together. You and Ray will stop by her house on the way to school."

Not even being closer to KiKi is making me feel better.

I can't believe Ray is just sitting here like he doesn't care that we're moving. What about the basketball hoop in our driveway that Dad got for him? Will that come to the new house? What about the height chart on the inside door of the hallway closet—will we have to start all over? And who's going to check on our neighbor Ms. Walters to see if she needs us to pick up anything while we're shopping at Target? Will there be anyone on our block who has a rose garden like she does? Will my new neighbors let me pick flowers for Mom as a gift for her birthday?

Mom looks at me and says, "Ryan, we'll all still be together. This is just a house. We are the ones who make it home. Home is wherever we go."

My ice cream is a pool of milk now and that's fine

with me because I *really* don't want it. Why would Mom and Dad ruin my favorite dessert? Don't they know that ice cream is supposed to be enjoyed on a hot summer day with the smell of sea salt water in the air, when the sun sits on top of the ocean waiting to be swallowed by the waves?

Here's the thing about ice cream. No matter how sweet it is, no matter if it's given to you even when you aren't supposed to have it, no matter if you're told you can come back for seconds—it doesn't take away the sadness.

SAYING GOODBYE

WE'RE GOING ON ONE last ride in Dad's Toyota. Later this evening, someone will come pick up the car and drive it away. So even though we don't really need to go anywhere, the four of us have piled into the car. Dad is driving, Mom is in the passenger seat acting as DJ, skipping all the songs Ray and I actually like. Ray is behind Dad, I'm behind Mom. "Where are we going?" Ray asks.

"Just a Sunday drive," Dad says.

We ride along the Columbia River and I start the car games we always play on family road trips. I point to a cluster of clouds. "That looks like a person running! See the two legs?"

"And that looks like a smiling face," Ray says.

We go on, finding cloud pictures, and then we start counting trees but there are so many, we both get tired of that, and so we decide to play my favorite game. Whenever we see a license plate that is not an Oregon plate we tag each other. If I get tagged the most, I'll have to do a chore that Ray gets to pick, so I try really hard to do most of the tagging. "California!" I yell. And right after, "Washington!"

"Not so loud," Mom says.

Then Ray tags me—hard. "Arizona, there's one from Arizona!"

"Okay, okay. Tag, not hit," I remind him.

We both call out another Washington plate at the same time. "I saw it first," Ray says.

"Did not."

"Yes, I did."

"It was a tie!"

"No—I saw it first and I tagged you first."

Dad looks at us through the rearview mirror. "If you're going to bicker, you'll have to stop playing."

I whisper, "You did not." And I tag him again—hard.

"Ryan Hart!" Dad yells. He was still looking at us and I didn't notice. I can't even deny hitting Ray, who is being all dramatic like I punched him or something.

Dad pulls off into a parking space and we all get out of the car. Ray runs around the car and yanks my hair. "That's for hitting me."

I push him. "That's for saying you saw Washington first—"

"Ryan and Ray, enough," Mom says. I don't know why she called my name first. Ray started it.

We stand looking out at the river. Mom pulls out binoculars from her tote bag. "Ryan, I see your loons and grebes." She calls them mine because diving birds are my favorite to watch. She hands me the binoculars. I see the birds resting in the water, their red necks glowing like fire flames.

Ray snatches the binoculars from me. "Look, a bald eagle! A bald eagle!"

Everyone is so fascinated with seeing the bald eagle, no one realizes Ray took the binoculars from me. Just pulled them right out of my hands. I am about to say something when Ray passes the binoculars back to me and says, "Sorry—but isn't this so cool? Look."

I look through the magnifying lenses and see that Ray is right. It is cool. And even though we've seen bald eagles before, it's always a magical thing to see them in the sky, dancing in the wind. I stand on one of the big rocks trying to get even closer to the clouds and Ray holds me up. "Be careful," he says. "You might fall." Even though I am not wavering at all.

On the way back home, Mom asks, "What do you want to listen to?"

Ray says one song, I say another.

Rock. Paper. Scissors. I get paper.

Rock. Paper. Scissors. I get rock.

Rock. Paper. Scissors. I get rock.

Even though I win, I choose the song Ray wants to listen to. I just wanted to be the one to decide.

We ride home listening to one of our favorite songs, singing along—even doing all the extra ad-libs. When we get home Dad parks the car on the street, not in the driveway like he usually does.

Everyone gets out except me.

For some reason I just want to sit here. Mom stands outside, at the foot of the steps, watching me, waiting for me. Maybe she is thinking that she is looking at this car one last time. Maybe she is remembering all the road trips to Seaside Beach, or riding around and around the parking lot at the zoo because no matter what time we go, there is never a place to park. Maybe she remembers the time she let us eat our McDonald's in the car (and we're never allowed to eat in the car) because everyone knows that cold french fries are the worst thing ever. Maybe she is thinking about how I'd store my books in the pocket in the back seat on the passenger's side, how she'd always say *pull out a book* whenever I said I was bored or if we were stuck in traffic and had to wait a long while. Maybe she is thinking about all the times I fell asleep on the way home from a place that wore me out so much Dad had to carry me inside, tuck me in.

I take a deep breath, take in the smell of vanilla—the scent Dad always gets for air freshener, candles, and incense. I get out of the car, close the door, and walk into the house with Mom. I know the car is not a person, but when we get to the door I turn around anyway and wave goodbye.

New Beginnings

THIS NEW HOUSE IS not new at all.

The front yard has not-that-green grass, like no one ever took care of it, and the screen door creaks every time it's opened. The not-so-soft carpet is tan and bland like food with no seasoning. The bedrooms are tiny and everything looks like someone used it before. When Mom shows me my bedroom, she says, "See, something good came out of moving." She smiles but I don't. I just go into my room, sit on my bed, and look out the window. There's a tree in the yard next door that is leaning over toward our house. The branches are reaching out, scratching my window.

This new house is not new at all.

Everything is on one floor, no stairs to climb like at our old home. Ray and I like to slide down the stairs, bumping up and down like we're sledding a snowy hill. Going up we'd see how many steps we could skip at a time. He always won because his legs are longer than mine. But here, there's only a narrow hallway with a ceiling light that doesn't shine bright.

This new house is not new at all.

The kitchen is too small for us to eat as a family. It is not even big enough to fit my sous-chef table—the one Mom bought me so I could help to cook alongside her in the kitchen. It's just a small plastic table tall enough for me to stand at without having to reach too high.

Mom says I'll make a good chef one day because I am always experimenting and thinking up unique concoctions. I didn't know what *concoctions* meant, so Mom made me look it up in the dictionary and I figured out that what she was saying is I'm good at mixing and inventing and putting foods together that may not normally go together but turn out so yummy and delicious and sometimes our favorite.

I am not old enough to cook by myself yet but Mom lets me help her. When I was younger, I had a pretend kitchen set right next to our kitchen and I played along as Mom made real dinner. Mom would act with me, make-believing that she was tasting my *concoctions*. As soon as I was old enough, she replaced the fake kitchen set with the small table so I could help with measuring and cutting.

Ray never helps in the kitchen, and when I used to play-cook, he never pretended to eat my concoctions. He only likes it when I have something real to feed him, like when Mom let me bake brownies with her using the real oven. We tried out one of my recipe ideas—lemon brownies. Ray thought lemons and chocolate were not going to taste good together, but when he went back for seconds I knew I had proved him wrong.

Mom thinks maybe one day I'll be a food critic. I didn't even know that was an actual job—to taste food and say if you like it or not. But I bet it is the coolest job to have. Sipping and tasting all day, telling people yes to this and no to that. Would my belly ache after eating so much food?

I ask Mom, "How am I going to cook with you without my sous-chef table?"

"Well, we'll have to find another way." She walks out of the kitchen and heads down the dark, long hallway.

I look around the house and see the chairs that are for the dining room table. I take one and set it at the kitchen counter, right next to the stove. I get on the chair sitting on my knees. The chair wobbles and I realize that this is not as comfortable as standing. I carry the chair back to the dining room and keep looking.

"Ryan, you need to help unpack. You can't just stand around," Dad says. He is carrying empty boxes into the dining room. "Please get the broom out of the closet and sweep the kitchen."

We've been busy all day getting the house set up

and unpacking. Everything has to be perfect because soon Grandma and her friend Mr. Simmons will be coming over for Easter dinner. Aunt Rose and Uncle David, too. We always have family dinners at our house, but that was because our house was the biggest. Even with moving, Mom insisted that we keep the tradition. I guess there are some things she doesn't want to let go of either.

I open the closet and take out the broom. I know Dad said to sweep, but before I do that I take out the step stool I find folded in the back of the closet. I open it and stand at the kitchen counter, right next to the stove. It's perfect. I will be able to cook with Mom and reach everything just fine. We'll cut and dice and measure together just like we always do. I think tonight we should cook one of our favorite dishes like we used to at our old house. But then I decide that since this is our first night here, I should try out a recipe we haven't had before.

Something in this place should actually be new.

WHAT NIGHT-LIGHTS ARE FOR

SOMETHING IS ON THE top shelf in my bedroom closet and I'm too afraid to open it.

I am standing on the stepladder trying to find a place to store the bin that holds my winter sweaters. The closet in my room is smaller than small, so I have to pack up some of my clothes to put away till I'm ready to wear them again.

I try one more time to get the bin to fit in my closet but I can't push it all the way back because there's a tin canister that's in the way. It looks just like the round cookie tin Grandma always has in her kitchen at Christmastime. "Ray, can you come help me?"

"Just a minute."

It takes more than a minute. But finally, Ray comes to my bedroom.

"Can you get that down for me?" I point to the canister.

"What is it?"

"I don't know."

"Whose is it?"

"I don't know."

"I'm not touching that!" Ray says. "I think we should leave it alone."

"But my bin won't fit unless we move it."

"You mean unless *you* move it." Ray steps away from the closet. "What if the person who lived here before left it there?"

"Well, if it was important, they wouldn't have left it."

"But what if the person who lived here died and the people who cleaned out the house had no idea that was even there?"

I've never thought about who lived here before us.

The thought that someone could have died here sends a chill through me.

Ray says, "If we open it, the man's spirit could haunt us."

"What if it was a woman who lived here?"

"I'm pretty sure it was a man."

"How can you know that?"

"I just know," Ray says.

I don't know why him saying this makes me want to open the canister even more. Maybe whatever is inside will prove that the person who lived here was a woman. I reach and reach and use my fingertips to inch the canister to the edge. Then I take it down, walk over to my bed, and open it.

Two seashells.

A postcard addressed to no one.

A white handkerchief embroidered with purple flowers.

Dried red rose petals.

Three gold hairpins all clipped on a small piece of cardboard with room for one more. It looks like someone took the fourth one off and never returned it. The hairpins are long and have a cluster of silver-tone flowers at the end. They are not everyday barrettes or hair clips. They look like something to wear on a special day, for a special reason.

"See, the person who lived here was a woman," I say.

"You don't know that." Ray steps closer to look at the items. He inspects them and then says, "Why do you think someone saved these shells?"

I shrug. "And why would someone have a postcard and not mail it to anyone?" And then, "I wonder what happened to the missing hairpin."

"Maybe she was wearing it when she died."

"Ray, stop trying to scare me!"

Ray laughs an evil laugh.

"Stop it, Ray. I mean it." I push Ray and he finally quits teasing me. I make up stories about the things we've found—fun stories that aren't creepy or sad. I tell a story about the most beautiful bouquet of roses the woman was given on her birthday. Maybe a big important birthday that marks a new decade of living, like forty or fifty or sixty or seventy or eighty. "It had to be an important occasion if she saved some of the petals," I tell Ray.

"*He*," Ray says. Just to annoy me, I'm sure. "What are you going to do with all of this?"

"I don't know. Put it on my dresser, maybe. These

shells are so pretty. They shouldn't be hidden in a dark closet."

"I think you should put everything back the way you found it," Ray says.

"You sound like you're scared. What, you think something's going to happen if I keep it out?"

"I think it's not yours so you shouldn't play with it."

"I'm keeping them," I say. I put everything back in the canister and set it on my dresser.

Ray walks out of my room. "Don't come crying to me when *his* spirit comes to haunt you."

I close my door, keep setting up my room, and try to forget about everything Ray said. I put the plastic bin of sweaters on the shelf, make my bed, and find a place to hang my nameplate. It's a sign with my name painted in yellow against a purple backdrop. One of the vendors at Saturday Market painted it and gave it to me as a gift. And it wasn't even my birthday or Christmas or any gift-giving day at all. She did it just because. Mom said those are the best kinds of gifts. I think so, too. I hang the sign above my dresser.

I don't really think about the canister for the rest of the day. Not until it's time to go to bed. All day long I have been so excited about having my own room and now that it is time, I'm a little nervous to sleep all by myself. I'd never tell anyone that, though. Especially not Ray.

Or Mom. She is in my room, helping me get ready for bed. "Honey, here's a night-light for your room. Just in case you get afraid tonight."

"I'm not a little girl anymore, Mom. I don't need a night-light," I say.

"Well, maybe just keep it in case it's too dark and you need to see how to get to the bathroom."

"I'll be fine. I don't need it."

Mom says okay and gives me her big Mom-hug, holding on a little longer at the end. "Good night. Love you."

"I love you, too."

Mom closes the door and I get into bed.

I don't know how long I've been asleep. All I know

is that a noise wakes me up. I can't tell where it's coming from. I lie real still, eyes opened wide, and listen for the sound again. Nothing. I turn over on my stomach, close my eyes, and try to go back to sleep. The noise comes again. It sounds like knocking or maybe footsteps. "Mom?"

No answer.

"Mom?"

More tapping.

"Ray? Ray, if that's you, you better stop it. You better stop trying to scare me."

The tapping continues.

"Ray?"

I think back to the tin canister we found. The seashells, the postcard with no note written on the back, the handkerchief and hairpins, the rose petals—hard and frozen in time.

Maybe Ray was right. Maybe the spirit of whoever lived here before is angry because we went through her things. Maybe she'll haunt me every night till I put them back where she left them.

"I'm sorry," I say out loud. "I'm sorry for going

through your belongings. Just please, please leave me alone. I promise to put them back. I promise."

"You promise?" a voice says. It's louder than a whisper but still soft and quiet.

I scream and pull the covers over my head. Then I hear loud laughter, and Ray's voice repeating what I said, mimicking me like a parakeet: *I promise to put them back. I promise.* He turns the light on and off, making it flicker like we're in a scary movie.

"Leave me alone!"

"I thought you didn't believe in ghosts. Who were you talking to?"

"Ray, get out of my room!" The whole neighborhood probably hears me.

Mom calls to us from her bedroom. "What's going on out there?"

Neither of us answers.

"Ray? Ryan?" Mom comes to my room, hand on her hip, hair tied in a silk scarf, bathrobe on, no slippers. She looks at me first. "What happened?"

I tell her the whole story. Starting with finding

the dead woman's things in my closet. And when I get to the part about Ray scaring me, Ray laughs like he's reliving the moment. And then instead of Mom telling him he ought to be ashamed of himself for being so mean to his little sister, she says, "Well, Ryan, I told you to sleep with a night-light."

"But having a night-light has nothing to do with Ray being a mean ole prankster."

Mom goes away, comes back. She walks over to my bed holding the night-light. "This way, Ray will keep out of your room. He can't hide in a room that isn't dark." She plugs in the light, turns it on. "Just use it tonight and if you want to keep it a little longer you can." Mom flicks the switch on the wall down and now it is dark with just a trace of light making a path along the carpet. "Both of you go to sleep. Not another word out of either of you." Mom yawns and walks back down the hall to her room. She doesn't even make Ray apologize. But when he drags out "Good niiiiight," she yells, "Ray!"

And that's that. He goes to his room and leaves me alone.

I lie in bed. The glow from the night-light is soft like moonlight. I don't really need it, but I'll keep it since it seems like Mom really wants me to have it. I'll keep it if it makes Ray stay out of my room.

FINDERS, KEEPERS

WE'VE BEEN LIVING IN the house for two weeks now and today I am having Amanda over for the first time. I promised Mom that Amanda and I would be quiet since Dad is sleeping. Now that he works all through the night, he sleeps most of the day, so we can't be too loud.

Amanda and I used to be neighbors at our old house but she moved last month to Lake Oswego, a place Dad says is too far and too white. Amanda goes to a different school now, so we don't see each other every day anymore. She's coming over—but just for a little bit while her mom runs a few errands in Northeast Portland.

Amanda and KiKi are my best friends. Sometimes we pretend we are cousins. Because we are best friends and because we are all in the fourth grade, we are always compared to each other. We have a lot of things in common, like our love of sour apple licorice, caramel corn, and glitter nail polish. But we have our differences, too. Amanda has an older sister and a younger one, too. KiKi is the only child and of course, there's me and Ray. My parents are Black and so are KiKi's. Amanda has a white mom and Black dad. KiKi has lived in the same house since she came home from the hospital. Amanda and I just moved. But Amanda's new house is actually new. No one has lived in it but her and her family. And it's bigger. Much bigger than my new (old) house. So I at least want to make my new bedroom cozy. *Cozy.* That's the word Mom uses to describe our new (old) house every time I start complaining about it being small. "It's not small, it's cozy," Mom keeps saying. Sometimes it sounds like she's trying to make herself believe her own words.

When Amanda gets here, I hug her real tight. I miss seeing her every day. We sit on the porch for a while, talking about her new school, her new friends. "It's not the same without you," she tells me.

"And Vernon is not the same without you," I say. "Me and KiKi miss you." I ask Amanda what she wants to do.

"You got any new recipes to try out?" she asks. Amanda is my official taste tester. She doesn't mind trying new things. And even if she doesn't like it, she doesn't make me feel bad like Ray does. He over-exaggerates every time he doesn't like something, spitting it out and running to get water to make the taste disappear from his tongue. His tongue that does not like spicy or too sweet, or tangy or tart. His taste buds hardly like any taste, so I mostly share my new concoctions with Amanda. She also helps me think up names for my creations.

"Mom, can we bake some of my new recipes so Amanda can try them out?"

"I'm afraid we don't have time for that, sweetheart. Amanda's mom won't be gone that long."

"Well, can I make my new smoothie recipe?"

"Sure," Mom says.

We pack the blender full of frozen blackberries, lime juice, plain Greek yogurt, and honey.

"Are you sure this is going to be good?" Amanda asks.

"I promise," I tell her.

Amanda looks like she's not so sure but once I pour the smoothie into her cup and she takes her first sip, I know she believes me. She asks for more before she's even finished. "Okay," she says. "What are we going to call this?"

"A blackberry-lime smoothie," I say.

"Come on, Ryan. That's too simple." Amanda takes a big gulp and says, "What about Blackberry Extravaganza?"

"But we can't leave out the limes."

"Okay, Blackberry-Lime Extravaganza?"

I don't really like that one, so I just keep sipping my drink.

"Or, Ryan's Berry-Lime Smoothie?"

I shrug.

"Okay, I'll keep thinking," she says. She turns the cup upside down and taps the bottom so she can have every last drop.

After we finish cleaning up the kitchen, I show Amanda my new room. Now that everything is put away, it looks nice and special and all mine. I don't even have to show Amanda the tin canister from the woman who might have died in this house. It's on the dresser and she notices it right away. "What's in there?" she asks.

I show her everything. "It's kind of creepy, right? But also cool."

Amanda touches everything gently, like sacred keepsakes. She picks up the hairpins, takes one, and sweeps a handful of her curly hair back, pushing it tightly in place.

"Does it feel weird?" I ask.

"Weird? No. Why would it feel weird?"

"Well, it might have been worn by someone who died here."

Amanda snatches the hairpin out.

I explain everything and tell her about the stories Ray and I made up.

Amanda puts the hairpins back in the canister and pushes the lid on. "I don't want to play with something that belongs to a dead person."

"But we're not even sure. It could be that the woman just forgot it. Maybe she moved away to a beautiful island because she's tired of all of Portland's rain. Maybe she's still living and sending postcards that actually have letters on the back to her family and friends."

Amanda doesn't look like she believes me. She looks scared. She backs up from my dresser and says, "I think you should throw the whole canister away."

"I'm not throwing this away. It's mine now. I found it, I'm keeping it."

"Girls," Mom calls out, "Amanda's mom is here."

I walk Amanda to the porch and wave to Mrs. Keaton. As soon as I close the front door, I start missing my friend. Ray is at baseball practice, so there's no one to keep me company. Not that Ray would want to play with me anyway. I go back to my room, sit on my bed, and look through my new (old) treasures. I didn't think twice about Ray being all paranoid about these things being possessed with the spirit of whoever they belonged to. But after seeing Amanda's reaction, I'm wondering if maybe I should throw them away. Get them completely out of the house so there's no chance of any ghosts coming to visit us. But then I think about what Grandma always says—there are no such things as ghosts. I put everything back inside, close the lid.

Pizza Night

Spring is here and the days are lasting longer and longer. I am trying a new recipe I got from one of the cooking shows I watch. It's not going exactly as planned.

"Something's burning," Ray shouts. He says this like we don't already know. Like he doesn't see me standing (on the step stool) next to Mom at the stove trying to help her peel the stuck chicken wings from the iron skillet.

"It's the rosemary," Mom says. "Maybe we should've added that last—or maybe we put too much."

My new recipe is a disaster. I wanted to make rosemary chicken wings with just a little lemon juice squeezed on top. But the rosemary is sticking and the pan started hissing like a furious cat when I added the lemon juice.

"It smells weird in here," Ray says.

"Shut up, Ray!" I grab the dish towel from the counter and swat at him.

"Enough, you two!" Mom takes the skillet to the sink. She rakes a spatula under the chicken, trying her best to save some of the meat.

"But Mom, Ray is the one coming in here starting stuff. It doesn't smell *that* bad."

"Yes, it does. It smells like smoke and burnt leaves and burnt chicken with a dash of burnt lemon." Ray laughs at his joke and Mom doesn't even say anything because she is so focused on rescuing dinner.

Dad comes into the kitchen, cell phone in his hand, giving Ray his stop-messing-with-your-sister look. "Honey, I'll just order pizza."

"No, Dad. I can try again."

Ray says, "I don't feel like waiting. I'm hungry now. Dinner was supposed to be done already."

"Nobody's even talking to you, Ray!"

Mom fusses at both of us. "I said *enough*." She looks at me and says, "Sweetheart, let's try this another night. It's getting late." She throws the burnt chicken into the trash. It looks more like charcoal than chicken. Mom doesn't think I hear her when she says "Like we have money to waste..." under her breath. She washes out the pan and tells Dad, "Call it in. Half pepperoni, half cheese."

"Yes!" Ray does a dance and says, "I love pizza night."

Mom puts her arm around me, says, "It's okay, Ryan. You just need to get used to this stove. It gets hotter faster than our old one. The oil was too hot, I think."

This new (old) house has ruined everything.

"Sorry I messed up dinner," I say.

Dad says, "Ryan, don't be so hard on yourself.

You're learning. No one expects you to get it right every time."

When the pizza comes, we grab our slices and head to the living room. Dad says, "Let's watch something on Netflix." We all gather to eat and watch a movie. We don't even need to break a tie because Ray and I want to watch the same thing.

Just before Mom pushes Play, I run back into the kitchen. "Hold on. Don't start yet."

"What are you doing?" Mom asks.

"Just adding a little more flavor to my pizza," I say. I sprinkle some of the rosemary on my slice of cheese. I've never tried this before. When I take a bite, it tastes so good.

AFRO PUFFS

MOST KIDS MY AGE are probably doing something really fun since it's Saturday, but not me. I am rehearsing my Easter speech over and over in my head so that tomorrow at church, I say it perfectly. Every Easter (and Christmas, too) all us kids who attend Sunday school recite speeches in front of the whole congregation.

This is the worst part of the holiday.

I hate everything about it: the way everyone stares, the way the microphone makes my voice sound weird, like I am underwater or speaking into an echo chamber, depending on who is working the sound system. I hate it because no matter how much I practice, I always forget a word and then I freeze and all the adults say *that's okay, baby* (even though I am not a baby), and all the other children, especially the teenagers, laugh. And then I just run off and hug Mom and she says, "It's okay. At least you tried."

This is what happens every year. But not this year.

This time I have read my speech so many times, I can say it in my sleep. This time I practiced in the mirror. This time I recited it as Amanda read along to double-check if I was saying it right. This time I will speak so loud, I won't even need the microphone. I will do so well, I will get a standing ovation.

This is what I am thinking about just before Grandma comes over to do my hair. She is coming to get me looking good for tomorrow because for our family, Easter is not only about speeches, it is about new spring dresses and Sunday shoes, every hair in place. It is about family dinner—deviled eggs, honey ham, mashed potatoes, mac and cheese, and collard greens. It is about wicker baskets full of chocolates and plastic eggs full of surprises.

When Grandma comes she hugs me and Ray and then walks through the house with Mom, who is showing her every room. "It's, um, it's . . . nice," Grandma says.

"Isn't it? The size adjustment took some getting used to but I don't think it's that bad. I think it's cozy."

"Yes, cozy. That's the word I was looking for," Grandma says. Grandma is a brown woman, tall like the sunflowers that rise in the community garden down the street. Nothing about her is small, or quiet, or timid. She goes into the kitchen and calls out to me. "Ryan, come on in here and let me fix you up." Grandma used to be a beautician. She owned a hair salon and made a living making women look pretty. She closed the shop last year but still does hair for special clients.

She is standing at the stove. When she turns it on, the fire blazes up and she adjusts the knob to make the fire settle to a low flicker. Grandma sets the pressing comb on the stove. The iron teeth of the comb begin to warm and just as smoke rises, I sit down in the chair in front of her.

She unbraids the thick twists Mom did after she washed my hair last night. Now my hair is dry and ready to be straightened. Most times I wear my hair in a big puffy ponytail. Sometimes Mom does two-strand twists and my hair hangs like the black yarn she uses when she sews dollies for her Saturday Market booth. I only get my hair straightened for special occasions. Grandma begins pressing my hair. "Child, there is no mistaking it. You are a Black girl and you have Black hair," Grandma says. She says this every time she presses my hair. "It is so thick. Just like your momma's." She pulls the comb through my kinky yarn and like magic, I feel the silky strands fall to my shoulders. "Weatherman says there's a chance of morning showers. But then clear and dry for the rest of the day. You know if it gets wet it will puff right back out and all this time spent straightening it will be a waste."

"Yes, ma'am," I say. Pressing hair takes a long time. I have to sit and sit and be very, very still, and hold my ear down so Grandma doesn't burn me as she straightens my edges. It takes forever, but I love the way it looks once it is all finished.

"You know, I used to do your momma's hair like this until she went natural," Grandma tells me. She pulls the pressing comb through my hair, then rests it on a towel sitting on the counter.

I can feel that one side of my hair is all straight and lying flat while the other side is still crinkled and all over my head. Ray walks into the kitchen and opens the refrigerator. "You look weird with your hair like that," Ray says. He pours cranberry juice into a cup and gulps it down.

"You look weird no matter how your hair looks," I tell him.

Mom calls out to us from the living room. "All right, you two. Don't start." She is sitting on the sofa knitting something to sell at Saturday Market. Next week the market starts back up, so she's been getting ready. Dad is resting before he has to go to work.

When Grandma is finished with my hair we go to the bathroom together. I stand in front of the vanity and she holds up a mirror behind me so I can see how I look. "I love it," I tell her. "I look beautiful."

"Well, Ryan," Grandma says, "you *are* beautiful. No matter if your hair is straight or not."

"Yeah, but I am more beautiful with my hair like this," I say. I run my fingers through my hair, feel them slip through every black strand. Instead of fuzzy yarn, it feels like silk.

Grandma turns me around to face her. "Baby girl, *you* are beautiful. Not just your hair or your clothes. But who you are. Your kindness makes you beautiful and the way you're always willing to offer help makes you beautiful," Grandma tells me. "And how creative you are with your recipes. That's what makes you a beautiful girl." Grandma turns me back to face the mirror. We both look into the glass, staring at my brown skin, my round face, my long straight hair. "How you wear your hair is your choice and no matter what you choose, it's not going to determine if you're beautiful or not. The only thing that will determine that is how you treat others. If you are mean to people, if you act ugly toward them, that's what takes your beauty away." Grandma kisses me on my forehead and then says, "Now let's get you ready for bed."

I put on my pajamas and my hair bonnet. Before I get into bed, I practice my speech one more time. I fall asleep holding on to Grandma's words.

WHAT EASTER MEANS TO ME

THE NEXT MORNING, MOM makes me wear a shower cap when I get in the tub. "So your hair doesn't get wet," she tells me. And when we go outside to get into the car to ride to church she tells me to put my hood on because it is drizzling.

Church starts off with prayer and singing. I usually sit next to Mom and Dad but today all the children who are saying speeches are sitting together. We take up three rows and will say our speeches in between songs the choir sings.

The choir sings their first selection and then Deacon LeRoy calls Luke up to the front of the sanctuary to play his piano solo. "Please give a round of applause for Luke as he plays 'Amazing Grace.'"

We all clap as Luke, who is sixteen, walks to the piano, sits down, and starts to play. Luke plays the piano like it was made just for him. His fingers float along the keys, making the old women cry and the old men lift their hands. And then, just as the adults start to really catch the Spirit, Luke turns around, winks at those of us in the front row, and starts to play the Linus and Lucy song from *Charlie Brown*. All of us kids start laughing and by the time Deacon LeRoy gets back to the microphone to get everyone to calm down, Luke has ended his piano solo and is returning to his seat.

"Well, ah, well, amen—that young man has a gift, doesn't he? Son, I hope you use your gift for good. Not to be mischievous." Deacon LeRoy clears his throat. "Now, um, let's see. Next we have Bobby Manning coming to recite his speech."

We are still giggling but then there is a hush over the audience once Bobby gets to the microphone. He is talking a little too fast but at least he says his whole speech. The mic wasn't turned up enough, so it was hard to hear him. Deacon LeRoy stands and says, "And next we have Miss KiKi." He adjusts the mic for KiKi and then motions to the sound man, pointing his thumb up, up, up. KiKi takes the mic off the stand and says her speech with no mistakes or pauses at all. She does so well, the whole congregation is clapping and saying amen. KiKi always does a good job. She is good at acting and singing and now I see making speeches is something to add to her long list of Things KiKi Is Good At.

After the choir sings two songs, Ray is next and of course he is perfect because he is good at everything. Then it's Gary's turn. Gary forgets one of his lines and starts crying so hard, his mom has to carry him off the stage. Olivia messes up twice, but she doesn't cry. Instead she keeps squinting her eyes. When I turn back to see what she is looking at, I see her mother mouthing the words. I turn back around and Olivia is leaning forward so far, trying to read her mother's lips, I think she might fall over. "Huh?" she says.

Her mother whispers—but not that quietly—"Christ rose on this day . . ."

"Huh?"

"Christ rose on this day . . ."

"I can't understand what you're saying," Olivia says.

Then Bobby blurts out, "Christ rose on this day!" And we all start laughing, even the adults. Olivia finishes her speech and runs back to her seat.

There are more speeches and more songs from the choir and then it's my turn.

I walk over to the microphone, feeling confident in my new dress with my freshly pressed hair. I speak the title loud, like I practiced, "What Easter Means to Me." The mic makes a high-pitched, squeaking sound and all the children in the front row plug their ears. I step back a bit and say it again, "What Easter Means to Me." The microphone isn't loud enough this time and some teen on the third row—who only comes to church on holidays with his grandparents—says, "We can't hear you!"

And Deacon LeRoy tells me, "Just take the mic off the stand. Hold it close to your mouth, sweetheart."

And I don't know if it's because my hands are sweaty or if it's because I just saw Olivia mess up so bad, but I drop the mic and it makes a really, really loud noise and now I have forgotten all the words to my speech.

"It's okay, baby, take your time," Ms. Howard says. She is the Sunday school teacher and the woman who puts on all special programs for Easter and Christmas and Youth Revival. "It's okay, just take your time," she says again.

I just stand there. I don't look at Mom or Dad or Ray or KiKi. I don't remember any of the words I practiced and practiced. I think maybe I can just say anything about Jesus and the cross and him rising, but Ms. Howard has our speeches in her hand. She is sitting there in the front row following along. Just when she starts to give me the first word, I walk away.

As I go to take my seat, I hear that holiday-church-going-boy say, "Guess Easter doesn't mean anything to her."

All the kids laugh and so instead of taking my seat, I keep right on walking. I see Mom scoot over to make room for me, like she did last year and the year before that, and always—but I don't go to sit by her. I go to my Sunday school classroom. I know no one will be in here. It's my favorite room in the church because of the pictures of brown angels that hang on the wall. I sit down on one of the metal chairs. I can't believe that after all that practicing, I got up there and could not remember my speech. Now that I'm in here all by myself, I can say it over and over in my head.

Mom comes into the classroom and puts her arms around me. She wipes my tears and gives me the same speech she always gives. "It's okay. At least you tried." She hugs me and says, "We ought to go back up and listen to the rest of the program."

"Please, Mom. Please don't make me go back in the sanctuary. I just can't."

"Now, Ryan, I think it's important that you go and support everyone else. Service is almost over. You won't be up there long. You can even sit with me and your father."

I can hear the choir singing and I know this means there is only one more round of speeches. "But Mom—everyone laughed at me. I don't want to go back up there."

"Ryan, honey, what have I told you about living up to your name? About being the leader you are?"

"I'm not a leader. I'm a girl who gets so scared standing in front of people that I freeze and forget my words. That's not a good leader at all."

"Yes, it is. As long as you tried. That's all I ask of you is that you try. You have nothing to be ashamed of. Next time, you'll try again and maybe you'll get through the whole thing." Mom takes my hand and we go back upstairs. "No holding your head down," she says.

I try. I really do try to keep my head up. But as soon as we go back upstairs, I keep my eyes on the floor, careful not to make eye contact with anyone. I wonder why Jesus's love for us has to be celebrated by torturing children to memorize poems. Right now, all Easter means to me is microphones that don't work and brains that forget words for no good reason.

After church, I rush to the car and don't even say goodbye or good job to KiKi. On the ride home Mom,

Dad, and Ray are all quiet and acting like if they say something to me, I will collapse into tears. Dad has the gospel radio station on and Kirk Franklin's voice is filling the car. I decide to say the speech out loud. I couldn't do it in front of a full congregation but I know I can do it here, with family. I know Mom is right about trying and trying and trying again. I ask Dad to turn the radio down and I begin.

What Easter Means to Me

It is the coming together
to give thanks, to sing praises.
Not for material things
but for the Love that heals us, that saves us.

It is the coming together
to embrace new beginnings,
to ask for and offer forgiveness,
to count our blessings,
to remember grace, to hold on to kindness.

Easter means a brand-new day
to try again, to lend a hand,
Easter reminds us to put others first,
to be the best that we can be.

This is what Easter means to me.

HOW TO MAKE A HOME

ONCE WE ARE HOME, I change out of my dressy clothes and put on a T-shirt and a pair of jeans. When I walk into the kitchen to help Mom finish cooking, she hands me an apron. I put it on, tie it tight, wash my hands, and start right away getting the deviled eggs ready.

Our new (old) house is too small to have this many here. There's Mom and Dad, me and Ray, Grandma and her friend Mr. Simmons, Uncle David and Aunt Rose, my cousins Ella and Micah, and two of my favorite people—Amanda and KiKi. Twelve people. Twelve hungry bellies and twelve bodies that need a place to sit. For formal dinners, we usually eat in the dining room but it's too small, so Mom says people will just have to eat wherever they find a place to sit. The grown-ups are in the living room. Everyone else is with Ray in his room playing video games.

Grandma comes into the kitchen. "Anything I can help you two with?"

"We're fine, Grandma."

"You sure?"

Mom says, "We're sure. You just rest. We're almost done. My little sous-chef is giving me all the help I need."

"Well, all right then," Grandma says. "Sure smells good in here."

I smile. I love when people tell me what I am making smells good, or when they take a bite and sing *This tastes sooo good*.

Once everything is warmed up, Mom and I bring out the food and set it in the middle of the dining room table. Dad calls everyone to the table so we can pray and then everyone starts passing plates and forks and napkins and food is being dished and before Mr. Simmons is back to his seat, he's taken a bite and says, "Oh my, what a feast."

He calls every dish out by name. "We've got deviled eggs, what is this—baked ham glazed with brown sugar? And look at these carrots. What's that drizzled on top?"

"Honey," I tell him.

"Hmm. Mac and cheese. Greens. Yes, Lord." Mr. Simmons sits in the living room on the sofa next to Grandma. They have been spending time together since the beginning of the year. Grandpa died five years ago, and I think it's nice that Grandma has a new friend who goes with her on walks through the park.

Mom calls everyone back into the dining room. We all crowd in and Mom says, "I just love gathering and spending time with all of you. Thank you for christening our home. This is our first time having guests over for dinner. I wasn't sure how it would be with all of us crammed in here, but to me this is perfect, all of us here together." Mom reaches her arms out to me and I walk over to her, taking her hand as she continues to talk. "I want to acknowledge this little one who helped me with every single dish. But this carrot cake? She pretty much made it all by herself. I just assisted." I can tell Mom is proud of me but I feel a little nervous, too. If no one likes this cake it will be my fault. I don't want my cake to fail as bad as my Easter speech did.

Mom cuts the cake and I hand out slices. KiKi gets the first piece because she is standing closest to me. "Mmm," she moans. "This is *soo* good." KiKi never fakes liking anything—not people, not food—so I know it is delicious.

We all eat our cake, some of us sitting and some standing. Once everyone is finished, Dad shouts, "It's time to hunt for the Easter eggs!" He walks out the back door and we all follow. "Whoever finds the most wins a special prize."

Amanda and Ray are the first out the door, then Ella, Micah, KiKi, then me. Before I even start searching, Micah yells, "Found one!" Amanda shouts,

"Found two!" Ella isn't calling out how many she's finding, but I see she has a few in her basket, so me and KiKi team up and decide to share the prize. KiKi finds a multicolored egg in the patch of grass next to the sprinkler. I find another one along the edge of the fence. We run around the backyard picking up eggs, laughing and screaming each time we find one. I can see that Ray has at least five. I have four. I spot a yellow egg at the back of the yard and run toward it. Just when I put my right leg down I hear *crunch*. When I look down, I see a pink pastel egg smashed into the grass. I bend over and pick up all the tiny shells, the crumbled boiled egg. By the time I finish the race is over.

"All right," Dad says. "Let's count it all up." He has us stand in a line side by side and counts our eggs one at a time. He comes to each of us and recounts them so he can make sure we found all of them. "Nothing worse than smelling a rotten egg stinking up the whole yard months after Easter," he says. "Amanda, your total count is nine. You're the winner."

Amanda's prize is the tallest Easter basket I've ever seen. Dark chocolate, white chocolate, milk chocolate, chocolate filled with caramel, chocolate filled with peanut butter. Chocolate hearts, chocolate bunnies. Even though it's all for Amanda, she says, "We can share," and sets the basket on the grass, sits down, and starts handing out candy. We all sit down in the grass and feast.

Once the sun starts to say goodbye and the evening sky comes, Mom calls us in and people start leaving. KiKi is the last one to go. Before she walks out the door she says to me, "I'm so glad you live closer to me now. This was so fun."

We hug and I tell her, "See you tomorrow." I close the door.

Mom and Dad are washing dishes in the kitchen. I join Ray in the living room straightening up, and I think about my family and friends and how Mom told me it's the people who make a place a home. Without love, all you have is a house. Mom is right about so many things.

WATER

ALL WEEK LONG I'VE been tying up my hair at night, wearing a shower cap in the tub, and pulling my hood over my head whenever I am outside. I am doing the best job at not getting my hair wet.

On Friday, Mom helps me pack for Amanda's birthday slumber party. I am almost finished getting ready when Mom tells me, "Don't forget your scarf and shower cap. And make sure you sign the birthday card. It's on the dresser." Then Mom looks the invitation over one more time and says, "Ryan, it says here to bring a swimsuit just in case you all go swimming. I'll pack your swimsuit but I don't want you getting in the pool, okay? You can sit on the side and get your feet wet, but no swimming. Your hair has only been pressed for a week. Let's keep it looking nice," she tells me.

"But Mom, I love to swim," I remind her. I took swimming lessons when I was three years old, and every summer we all go to Matt Dishman Community Center and swim during the Family Swim hour.

"Ryan, I am serious. You hear me? You better not get in that pool."

"Yes, ma'am," I say. I don't even say it in a pouting voice because I know if I do Mom might say I can't go at all. And that would be worse than not being able to swim.

On the way to Amanda's all I can think about is the fun we are going to have. I wish KiKi were coming. She's at her dad's for the weekend, so she's missing out on all the birthday fun.

I wonder what we'll do first—eat birthday cake (chocolate, I hope), watch a movie, or maybe have a dance party?

I wonder who will be the first one to fall asleep and who will be the last.

I wonder how many other friends Amanda invited.

I wonder if Amanda's new friends will like me.

I wonder if I will be the only brown girl.

I wonder if they will think I am weird for not getting in the pool.

We pull up to Amanda's new house. It looks nothing like her old house. It is wider and taller and everything looks better than what I have at my house. Mom drops me off with kisses and says, "I'll pick you up tomorrow afternoon."

The first thing Amanda says to me is, "I'm so glad you're here."

Zoe, Amanda's younger sister, runs and gives me a hug. She is five. "It's Amanda's birthday," she tells me. Like I don't know. I smile and hug her back.

Amanda introduces me to everyone. There are

four other girls—Haley, Caitlin, Red, and Sophie. All the girls are white except Sophie. She is brown, too, and much lighter than me, with curly hair like Amanda's.

We spend the first hour dancing to one of Amanda's new video games where you can hold the control and follow the steps on the screen. We're all pretty good at dancing, except Red, who is getting more and more frustrated the more points me and Haley get. Zoe is in the way—dancing wild and not even following the guide. Mrs. Keaton takes her to her playroom. "Come on, I'm going to put on a movie for you to watch," she says, and they disappear.

We eat pizza and drink so much soda, my belly is tight. Then we sing happy birthday and eat cake (not chocolate, but still good). Red complains that my slice of cake is bigger than hers and it is but not by much and anyway, who is she to make such a big deal about whose slice is bigger? It's not her birthday and if Amanda doesn't care, she shouldn't care. And so while she's going on and on about her slice being smaller than mine, while she's not looking, I slide an even smaller piece close to her and exchange it, so now she really does have the worst slice that was cut. There's not that much frosting on it, either. Haley sees what I've done and smiles at me.

Red doesn't even notice because she's talking and talking about me and Amanda—about a friendship she knows nothing about. She says, "Who is Ryan, your best friend or something?"

Amanda says, "Yes. She is. I've known her since the second grade. We lived on the same block."

"Well, you don't live on the same block anymore," she says. "You two barely see each other. How can you be best friends?"

"It doesn't matter where your friends live. Home is not about—"

"Uh, yeah, it does matter. And I live right across the street. I spend time with Amanda every day. We walk to school together, we walk home from school together. We hang out on weekends."

I wish KiKi were here. I wish Amanda's birthday

party was like last year. Just Amanda and KiKi and me. Three friends is enough.

Good thing Amanda's mom calls to us. "Girls, let's get ready for the swimming pool!"

Red runs to change into her bathing suit and everyone is acting like she didn't just say the meanest thing to me. But it doesn't matter now. We're all changed and we're going to have fun at the pool. I have never been in a house that has its own indoor swimming pool. I think if I lived in a house like this, I would swim every single day and not just in the summer.

Mrs. Keaton is in a bathing suit, too, but she doesn't get in the pool. She is lying on a lounge chair reading a book. She says, "There are floaters if anyone wants to use them." Everyone knows how to swim, so no one gets any of the foam noodles. Amanda's older sister, Melissa, is in the pool with us. She is seventeen and she used to be a lifeguard at the community center until they moved. I wonder if she volunteered to watch us or if Mrs. Keaton is making her. Melissa sees me sitting on the edge of the pool and calls over to me. "You don't want to join us?"

"No, thank you," I tell her. I don't say anything about my hair, just dip my feet in the water and kick up a gentle splash.

But then Red backstrokes over to me and says, "What's the matter? Scared of the water?"

She doesn't give me a chance to tell her how good a swimmer I am and how every summer I go to the pool.

"It's not that deep," Red says, pointing to her right. "If you stay on that side, you can stand up in the water. Don't be a scaredy-cat."

"I'm not a scaredy-cat," I tell her.

Red shrugs and whirls away and joins the other girls who are all playing Marco Polo. Sophie is trying to tag someone and every single time she gets close to Amanda or Caitlin, she misses. It's so funny to watch her waving her hands from side to side, almost reaching them but not.

Finally, Sophie tags Red and then all of a sudden Red is tired of playing. "Why don't we do something else?" she says. I think she says this because she doesn't want to be It. Red says, "Let's see who can hold their breath underwater the longest." She swims closer to the girls. They huddle and wade in the water. "Whoever wins is Amanda's new best friend." Red looks at me when she says this. "Too bad you can't swim, Ryan."

"I can swim!"

"Well, you're not in the water and that means you're not Amanda's best friend anymore. What kind of person shows up to her best friend's birthday party and refuses to play with everyone else?"

I am not going to let some girl named after a color in the rainbow tell me I am not Amanda's best friend. I get up, go into Amanda's bedroom, and take my scarf and shower cap out of my suitcase. I know Mom said not to go swimming, but this is technically not swimming. Plus, I am tying my hair up like I do at night *and* wearing my shower cap like I do in the tub. Double protection. My hair won't get that wet, will it?

I rush back out to the pool and get in.

"We can have the contest," Amanda says. "But it's not about being my best friend."

Yes it is. I can tell Red is serious and so am I.

Once I get in the water, Red says, "Okay now, who can hold their breath underwater the longest? Ready? One . . . two . . . three . . . go!"

The six of us sink our heads into the water. Our eyes get big and mine begin to sting, but I stay underwater. Haley is the first to pop up and then Caitlin. Sophie is next and I can't believe it but Amanda is right after her. I thought she might beat us all, which would be funny if she won being her own best friend.

It gets down to me and Red.

I close my eyes and hold on a little longer. And in a few seconds I hear the water splash and realize Red has given in.

I won! I won! I leap back up on top of the water and I am ready to celebrate. I am Amanda's best friend. I will always be Amanda's best friend. I expect Amanda to be smiling and maybe Caitlin,

Sophie, and Haley, too. But instead of smiles and cheers, they are all just staring at me.

"What happened to your hair?" Haley asks.

I lift my wet arm and feel around my head. My scarf and shower cap are not there. They are floating in the water. My hair is wet and I can't see it but I know it isn't straight anymore. I can tell by how fluffy it feels when I squeeze it.

All of the other girls' hair is wet, too, but the white girls' hair is slick and straight now that it's wet. The water makes Sophie's and Amanda's curly hair even more curly.

"Your hair looks like it got electrocuted!" Red says.

I rush out of the pool, grab my towel, and go to the bathroom. I stand in front of the mirror, dripping wet from the pool and my tears. I dry off and sit on the floor. I can't go back out there. Some of my hair is straight, some of it is puffy. I remember what Ray said about my hair looking weird and Red's voice, too.

Melissa knocks on the door and asks me if I'm okay, but I don't answer.

Mrs. Keaton knocks on the door and asks me if I'm okay, but I don't answer.

Then Amanda comes to the door.

She doesn't knock or ask me if I'm okay. She just sits on the floor. I know it's her because she is the only one here who knows that when I'm upset, I don't want to talk about it. I can hear her breathing and I know she'll sit and sit there as long as I am in here. I don't want her to miss her party and I don't want the other girls to think I'm a crybaby.

I stand close to the door and whisper to Amanda, asking her to go into my suitcase and bring me my comb. She leaves and comes back and I open the door and let her in.

I stand in front of the mirror and I really just want to start crying all over again. Now that my hair is drying, it is even more puffy and ridiculous looking. I stare at myself and my tangled hair and try to remember what Grandma said about beauty. I think maybe I acted ugly today—wanting to prove Amanda was my best friend, swapping Red's cake, and wanting to show off.

Red is at the door now, knocking and saying, "Amanda, come on. You can't stay in there and baby her all night. Why are you two even friends?"

Amanda says, "We just are." And leaves it at that. And this makes me love Amanda even more and lets me know that no matter where we live or how big or small our houses are, we will always be friends.

I am not good at twisting my hair but I am good at combing through it. Mom always has me comb through it before she washes it. I part my hair into four sections, like Mom taught me, and I comb through it. I wet the comb and go through each section a second time. Now all of my hair is big and full and not flat at all. Amanda gives me a rubber band and I pull my hair into it, making a big, big Afro puff.

I don't wait for a compliment from Amanda. I like the way my hair looks. And this way, I don't have to worry about water—the shower, the rain, or the pool. I like the way my hair looks like one massive storm cloud, how if I stretch it, it boings back into place.

I don't know what kind of trouble I'll be in when Mom finds out what happened and I feel bad that Grandma wasted her time, but right now, I try not to think about that. I walk out of the bathroom with my best friend and my natural hair and I try to be the beautiful person Grandma says I am.

HANNAH WILKERSON HAS TALENT

MOM DOESN'T FUSS AT me too much when she comes to pick me up. Maybe because everyone is watching. She just takes me in her arms and says, "I'll do your hair when we get home." Parents are so strange sometimes. The way they get so mad about things that you think are no big deal but then, when you are holding your breath in fear of what consequence might come, they don't say a word.

Mom does my hair as soon as we get home. She twists it and says, "Now you can do all the swimming you want." She oils my scalp with coconut oil and tells me, "And the next time I tell you not to do something, you need to listen. Okay?"

"But I wasn't swimming," I tell her. "I just got in the water to see who could hold their breath the longest."

"Ryan, I told you not—"

"But this girl named Red—what kind of name is that?—kept being mean to me and—"

"Is that what happened? You were showing off? So you didn't even get into the pool to have fun and swim?" Mom is finished with my hair, so I get up from the floor and turn to face her. She looks upset. More upset than when she came to pick me up. "Ryan, you don't ever have to prove yourself. I want you to be your best for you, not to show off. You understand?"

"I understand," I say.

On Monday, everything is back to normal. School actually went by fast today and that never, ever happens. I walk with KiKi to meet Ray. We pass the multipurpose room (they call it this because sometimes it's a place where we have assemblies, and sometimes the room is used for indoor recess on rainy days, or meetings for teachers and so many other things).

There is a sound coming from the room.

The sound is calming like wind chimes gently dancing in a summer breeze.

The sound is big and fills every inch of the hall-way, like rainbows do when they take over the sky.

The sound is Hannah Wilkerson.

She is the best singer at Vernon school, even

though our teachers never say it. They say silly things like, *If you can talk you can sing* and *Everyone has a voice*, and I know that's true but not everyone has a voice like Hannah's. When she sang a solo at last year's holiday celebration, she got a standing ovation.

No one ever stands or cheers when I sing.

Hannah is a big girl with dark brown skin. Her hair is always in tiny, long braids that drape down to the middle of her back. She is always dressed in the most stylish outfits. I stand at the door and listen, peeking in so I can see. There she is, standing with perfect posture, just like Ms. Warren teaches us. KiKi says, "I don't like her."

"Why?"

"Because she thinks she's all that."

"All what?"

"All *that*," she says, pointing at Hannah. "She thinks she's the best singer, the best dressed, the best looking."

"Did she say that?" I ask.

"Of course not," KiKi says. "But I know she thinks it."

KiKi isn't making much sense to me. "Well, how do you know she thinks that?"

"I just know. I can tell," she says. We listen to Hannah a little more, even though we are supposed to be going outside to meet Ray so we can walk home. Just before KiKi turns away, she says, "Can't you just tell?"

"Yeah. I can tell," I say. "She thinks she's all that." The words feel strange coming out of me. Like when I taste something that I don't like, but I eat it anyway.

We walk away, leaving behind Hannah's perfect everything. I ask KiKi what she's going to do for the talent show. She says, "Nothing."

"You mean you're not going to be in it? I thought all fourth graders have to be in it." As soon as we get outside I squint because the sun is too much sun.

"Well, I'm not in it, I'm hosting it. Ms. Barnes asked me to be the MC—Mistress of Ceremonies," KiKi says. "I'd rather do that than stand onstage and perform for everyone."

I see Ray standing outside in the place where we always meet.

We start walking, making our way home, Ray on the outside of the sidewalk, closer to the curb, like Dad taught him. I am in the middle of him and KiKi, which is the worst place to be when KiKi says, "So, Ryan, what is your talent going to be?"

"Well, I'm good at cooking."

"That's not the kind of talent you can do at a talent show," Ray says.

KiKi agrees and then it starts—the two of them going back and forth about how cooking is not a talent. Ray laughs and says, "I mean, you could maybe win a cooking show but there's no way you're going to win against singers and dancers."

"But it's a talent show. Not a competition. And we should do what we're good at," I say.

"There's a prize," KiKi says. "It's definitely a competition."

"I remember doing that when I was in the fourth grade," Ray says. And he emphasizes *fourth grade* like it was so long ago, like he's so much older than us. "I won," he tells us.

"You did not," I say. Even though I am not sure.

"I did too. I did a rap with two of my friends and we won."

KiKi asks, "Was there a prize?"

"Free passes to the movies and something else, but I can't remember."

I walk home in the blinding May sun between Ray and KiKi. The two of them have moved on to talking about something else, but I'm still trying to think up a talent other than cooking.

I'm thinking maybe I don't want to do this talent show. I am not like Hannah, or KiKi or Ray. KiKi is confident enough to get up in front of a full auditorium and talk and smile and introduce people, making everyone feel good and happy to be in the room. And there's Hannah with her standing ovations. And there's Ray, whose teachers are always saying how smart he is—always getting high scores on his science and math tests. He's the best baseball player in the sixth grade and he's good at rapping and putting songs together.

Ray has so much talent. Winning a competition is

no big deal to him. He doesn't even remember the prize. I don't understand how anyone can forget something so special. I guess people with so much talent don't remember when they are acknowledged for it. I wonder if Hannah is that way. I wonder if she'll win the talent show and two years from now not even remember what she won, or what song she sang. Maybe it's no big deal to them because they are not trying to show off. Maybe they do what Mom says I should do—be their best for themselves, not for others, so even if they don't get the award (but they almost always do) they will still feel proud because it was something they had fun doing.

I understand what Mom is telling me. But does she understand how hard that is?

SATURDAY MARKET

SOMETIMES MOM LETS AMANDA come with us when she works at her Saturday Market booth. Mom shares the booth with Millie, a woman who sells handmade soaps and lotions. Besides Mom, Millie is one of the only Black vendors at the market. There's also Paul, the man who sells the most beautiful paintings of Portland landscapes. Every time I go to his station, he gives me a Moonstruck chocolate and says, "You know Moonstruck is local. Best chocolate in the world." I always act like I am hearing it for the first time.

In fall and winter months, Mom sells the hats,

gloves, and scarves she knits, but in the spring and summer, she knits purses and wallets and all kinds of bags. "Set these over there," Mom says, pointing to the long table that's draped in African kente. The green, blue, and yellow blend into a beautiful print that makes the table look like a piece of art. I put the box of merchandise on the table and start unpacking. Amanda helps me organize everything by color and size. When we're finished, Mom says, "Be back in an hour to check in. Stay close." And with that, Amanda and I are free to roam the aisles of the market, looking at jewelry and stopping by the main stage to listen to the live bands play. We go back every hour to let Mom know that we are okay and then she sends us out again.

The third time we walk through the market, Amanda says, "Want to get a snow cone and an elephant ear?"

"Maybe just an elephant ear," I say. It's not that I don't want both, it's just that Mom only gave me enough money to get one treat. We walk over to the stand that is selling blended coffee drinks and elephant ears. I say to Amanda, "Remember the first time you had elephant ears?"

Amanda starts laughing. "I thought you and Ray were so gross. I couldn't believe you were actually eating the ear of an elephant. But then I tasted it and realized what it was."

"The best thing ever! Fried dough sprinkled with cinnamon. Big and flappy just like elephant ears. My favorite treat to get at the zoo and here at the market," I say. As we inch up in the line, I can smell the warm dough more and more. I inhale as much of the cinnamon-filled air as I can.

Amanda says, "I think every person in the world should have an elephant ear at least once."

And as soon as she says this, I blurt out, "That's it! That's what I'll make for the talent show. I'll give the judges different kinds of spreads to put on top—caramel, marionberry jam, and chocolate. No one will deny that it's the most delicious thing they've ever tasted."

"You will definitely win. Especially if you set up the stage like this and make it feel like they're all at Saturday Market."

"Yes!"

It's our turn to order and when we do I ask for an extra plate and extra, extra napkins because eating elephant ears is messy. The cinnamon crystals get all over my shirt and lips and fingers but it's worth it.

Amanda and I pull the fried dough apart as we walk and eat the gooey goodness on our way back to Mom's booth. Our mouths are too full to talk, so we just walk, side by side, eating and licking our buttery fingers.

When we check in with Mom, she is almost out of merchandise, so I know we won't be here much longer. Instead of going off too far, we just walk across the aisle to the stand with the sign that says Scarves & Things because Amanda wants to see the scarves up close. Amanda starts draping herself in the silk material—around her neck, as a headband, on her waist. A thin boy, who's maybe a teenager helping out, walks over to her and holds a mirror up so she can see herself. While she's trying on this one and that one, I look at the table of rings and bracelets. They all look like antique things—something made a long, long time ago. I walk along the table and then I see something that almost makes me scream Amanda's name but I catch myself. Instead, I just stare at it. It's a hairpin. A hairpin that looks just like the ones I discovered in the tin on the shelf in my closet, with the same silver cluster of flowers.

"Would you like to try it out?" a woman asks me. She is a chubby woman with brown curly hair. She picks it up and hands it to me. The moment it's in my hand I know it's the missing hairpin.

Without me even realizing it, Amanda is behind me asking, "What are you looking at?" She doesn't see what's in my hand at first, so I hold it out to her. "Isn't that the same—"

"Yes, well, yeah, I think so."

Amanda looks at me, then back at the woman.

The woman says, "This belonged to my grandmother. Isn't it lovely? Really, go ahead—try it on."

Amanda grabs my hand. "That's okay, we . . . ah, we have to get back to her mom's booth." Amanda takes the hairpin out of my hand, puts it back on the table, and drags me away before the woman can say anything else. "That was creepy. Do you think she's a ghost?"

"No. Not at all. She's real. She's definitely real." My heart is jumping and Amanda's hand is sweating. When we get back to Mom, we both talk at the same time saying, "Guess what happened," and "You're not going to believe this." I start telling her all about the woman we met and how she has a hairpin that matches the ones I found in the closet.

But Mom isn't as excited about our news. She is ready to pack up and needs help. "Here, put these in that crate," she says to me. And to Amanda, "Can you fold the tablecloth?"

I say, "Mom, did you hear us? I think we just met the granddaughter of the woman who lived in our house. She had the same—"

"Ryan, honey, those hairpins are a dime a dozen. They're not as precious as you think."

"But Mom—"

"It would have to be a really big coincidence for that woman to have any connection to the house we moved into."

"But Mrs. Hart, I really think Ryan is right."

Mom says, "Here, sweetheart, put the tablecloth in that crate."

When we say goodbye to Millie, she gives us each a small soap that smells like grapefruit. Amanda and

I keep talking about how the woman and the hairpin and our new (old) house must be connected. Halfway home, Mom gets tired of hearing our tales. "Can you two please talk about something else? Anything else?" she asks.

And so for the rest of the ride, I tell Mom how I plan to make elephant ears for the talent show, but she doesn't seem too excited about this conversation, either.

JOY, SWEET JOY

DAD KNOWS EVERYBODY IN Northeast Portland. Well, not everybody, but he knows a lot of people because he worked for fifteen years delivering mail to our neighbors and to the businesses around the community. Everywhere we'd go people waved and said, "Hi, Mr. Hart," and sometimes they joked around with him and asked, "Got any special deliveries for me?" even though he wasn't in his uniform. He usually laughed and said, "Not today. Maybe next time."

But now when people call out to him he just says, "Not today," and he leaves off the part about there being a next time because there will be no chance of a next time. After the post office he worked at closed, he couldn't be transferred because there were no positions open in other districts. I don't understand how a post office could close. Everyone needs their mail delivered. But when I said this to Dad he said, "People don't rely on the post office like they used to."

It makes me sad to know that Dad is really good at doing something people don't need him to do anymore. This is one reason why I think being a chef is the best thing to be. People will always need food.

And speaking of food, ever since Dad lost his job we haven't been able to buy the same kind of groceries. Even though he is working again, it doesn't pay the same. So today while we shop at Fred Meyer, I try to remember not to ask for anything that isn't already on Mom's grocery list. Like my favorite cereal. Mom bends down and gets a box from the bottom shelf—the whole row is full of cereals that look like the name-brand flavors but taste so different.

I don't complain about that. Or the cheese, or

yogurt. But when we get to the ice cream aisle, I can't help it. "What flavor should we get?" Mom asks. She opens the freezer that's full of Kroger's brand. Not Tillamook or Ben & Jerry's.

"Chocolate. But can we get Tillamook instead?"

"That's too expensive, Ryan."

"Well, what about Ben & Jerry's?"

"Ice cream is ice cream," Mom says. She puts a half gallon of Kroger's chocolate ice cream in the shopping cart.

I know to Mom it doesn't really matter. But I think Ben & Jerry could teach whoever Kroger is a few things.

The one thing Mom splurges on is coffee. Stumptown. "Can you grab that, please?" she says, pointing to a bag of ground coffee beans. I take the bag off the shelf and put it in the cart next to the box of assorted Top Ramen noodles. "A man deserves a good cup of joe in the morning." Mom is talking to herself this time. She says this every time she buys a new bag.

This is how it is now. No more name-brand food,

or clothes, or soap, or lotion. Everything we buy is on sale and now grocery shopping takes a long, long time because instead of going to one store, we shop at two or three depending on what Mom has a coupon for.

After we leave Fred Meyer, we go to Safeway to take back our soda cans. Mom always gives me the money we get from returning our cans so I can buy any special spices or ingredients for new recipes I want to try. Safeway has all the things I need, so we do the can return here. When we get out of the car, Mom unlocks the trunk and takes out two big plastic bags of cans. There's a long line today because two out of four of the machines are out of order. There's a man with five full garbage bags of cans and bottles. We are going to be here for a while.

Mom sighs. "Sorry, Ryan."

"For what?"

"Just . . . I'm just sorry we even have to be in this line."

"I don't mind waiting," I say.

Mom doesn't seem to be listening. She looks like her mind has taken her someplace else. Her eyes are sad and I don't know what I should do or say, so I take Mom's hand because whenever I am really sad, I like for Mom to hold my hand.

Once we finally get to the machine, I start passing the cans to Mom and she tosses them in. The machine gobbles the aluminum, making a *crunch ... crunch ... crunch* sound. Flies are circling around our heads coming for the sweetness in the cans. My shoes stick to the ground and every time I move, it's like glue is keeping me in place.

"We're almost done," I tell Mom.

"Huh?" she shouts over the loud machines.

"We're almost done," I repeat. Maybe too loud this time, because the woman behind us hears me and says, "Well, thank God for that. People got things to do." I look back and see that the line has doubled and people are standing with their hands on their hips, huffing and puffing. Some are on their cell phones, others are just standing still and looking straight ahead.

And then I see her. Hannah. The girl with the voice of angels. She is in line standing next to an older woman, maybe her grandmother. Seeing her here makes me think about what KiKi said—that Hannah thinks she's all that. Seeing her here makes me think that maybe there's a lot about Hannah that we don't know.

I wave.

She waves back.

I reach toward the machine and toss the can in. "Last one," I say.

Once we are home, we start making dinner together. I can hardly focus because Dad and Ray are distracting me by making funny noises and silly faces when Mom isn't looking. She fusses at us.

Dad says, "Oh, a little fun never hurt nobody." He takes Mom's hand. "Can I get a beat, Ray? I want to serenade my lady."

Ray takes his spoon and taps it on an empty pot making a rhythm, then he starts beat-boxing. Dad starts rapping and now Mom is laughing and moving her shoulders. They are both dancing and I join in singing a melody and it sounds like we really know how to make a song.

But then Ray drops his spoon.

The rhythm stops, so we all stop.

"My bad, my bad." For once Ray messes something up.

We all start laughing and Dad says, "If I don't find a better paying job soon, maybe we should take this show on the road. The Hart Family on tour. I like the sound of that."

We laugh and laugh. And that's one thing that hasn't changed.

RACING BEES

IT'S SATURDAY AFTERNOON AND I'm bored. Ray is leaving to race bikes with his friends at Alberta Park. I beg to go. "Mom, please can I go with Ray?"

Ray says, "I don't want to babysit."

"First of all, I am not a baby. And also, I can invite KiKi and that way, you don't even have to play with me."

Mom likes this idea. "If KiKi is going, you can go, too, Ryan. Ray—look out for your sister."

Ray hands me my helmet and says, "Make sure you keep up with me."

Like I need him to tell me that.

Then he says, "And put your helmet on."

Even though I am going to put it on right after I double-check my shoelaces. I want to make sure they are tied so they don't get tangled in the chain while I'm riding.

"Hurry up," Ray says. "Logan and Aiden are already there waiting for me."

We ride to Alberta Park, Ray in front and me right behind him. Around the corner from my house is an apartment building with the most beautiful tree in front of it. When Ray and I ride our bikes past the tree, I slow down just a bit so the branches that are hanging low and stretching down to the ground can hug me. The wind touches my face, gentle and soft, like Mom's hands rubbing my back when I'm sick.

"Keep up!" Ray shouts.

We keep riding and as we approach the end of the block, Ray says, "Start slowing down."

I was already slowing down. I can see that we're at the end of the sidewalk. But I know Ray is just doing what Mom and Dad told him to do: protecting me.

We are the last ones to get to the park. KiKi is sitting under a tree listening to music and reading. She doesn't have a bike. She says it's because she doesn't like to ride but I know it's because she never learned how to ride a bike without training wheels.

When we get to the park, Logan and Aiden are racing each other up and down the steep hill. Logan tags the tree at the top and does a somersault to show off that he won.

Aiden picks up his bike from the ground and says, "That doesn't even count. We came here to race bikes. Bet you can't beat me riding up that hill."

And now the official competition has started.

Ray says, "Aiden and Logan round one. I'll race the winner."

And then I say, "And I'll race the winner of round two."

"You're supposed to be hanging out with KiKi," Ray reminds me.

"I am. I'm hanging out with KiKi until I race whoever wins round two."

Logan and Aiden get on their bikes and Ray counts them off. Aiden is a much faster bike rider than he is a runner. Logan is far behind. It doesn't even seem like a race. When it's Ray's turn, I already know he is going to win. One reason is because he is really fast. Another is because Aiden is really tired now.

Ray wins.

"My turn, my turn!" I shout. I get on my bike and ride to the bottom of the hill.

Ray looks at me. "I'm not going to go easy on you," he says.

"Good." I tighten my helmet.

KiKi shouts, "On your mark, get set . . . go!"

I pedal as fast as I can. The first part of the hill is hard because it's so steep. Ray is right next to me. We keep up with each other the whole way but then the hill straightens and I don't have to pedal as hard. I go even faster and I'm ahead of Ray—not by much, but I'm ahead.

I shout out to him, "Don't let me win on purpose!"

"I'm not. I'm tired. I just raced Aiden."

I believe him and I make myself go faster and faster.

Here I am at the top of the hill. I won. Ray is just one second behind me, but still. I won. And I didn't fall! I don't even gloat, I just bend and put my hands on my knees and try to catch my breath.

"Good race," Ray says. No enthusiasm in his voice, but at least he acknowledged that I beat him.

I take my helmet off and toss it. I'm sweating and out of breath and I don't even realize how hard I threw my helmet until KiKi says, "Your helmet got stuck in that bush."

I walk over and see my purple-and-yellow helmet stuck in the middle of the bush. I reach in the middle and try to shake it loose. That's when I realize this isn't an ordinary bush. This is a bush that has a bee-hive in it and I've just shook the hive. Bees start swarming all over my arm, my head.

I scream and swat at them.

"Be still," Ray says. "Be still." He runs over to me.

Not moving is impossible. I am not going to stand here and get stung by a million bees. Some are hovering around me like a halo, and even more are buzzing around my ears. I am crying now. KiKi is using her book to swat at them but it's not helping.

Ray just keeps yelling, "Be still. Be still."

But I can't, so I take off running. First in a circle but then I decide to run home. I want Mom. I am sure the bees are chasing me, like they are playing a game of tag. I try to outrun them, crying and screaming the whole way home.

When I get to my house, I bang on the door and ring the doorbell over and over until Mom is standing in front of me with panic in her eyes. "Ryan, honey, what's wrong? What happened?"

I am crying too hard and I'm too out of breath to talk, so KiKi says it all and this is the moment I realize KiKi ran behind me, that she has my bike and helmet. Ray, Logan, and Aiden are here, too. Everyone is sweating and breathing hard.

Mom checks my body, looks through my twists,

shakes out my shirt. "You're okay. You're okay. They're gone. They're gone. It's a wonder you don't have stings all over you."

Slowly, my breath calms and steadies. I can feel my heart relaxing in my chest, going back to its normal rhythm. *I'm okay. I'm okay.* And out of nowhere, we all start laughing. Me, the hardest. Today, I not only beat my brother in a bike race. I outran a team of bees.

16

SECRET INGREDIENTS

SUNDAY, INSTEAD OF GOING to church, Mom says she
needs a day to rest. "Sometimes, you just need a day
to do nothing," she says. And she goes into her bedroom and stays there most of the day.

Ray and I mostly watch television—and this is
how I know Mom is really tired. She never lets us sit
and watch TV all day. We've been watching a teen
chef competition for the past hour and even though
there are more episodes, Ray takes the remote and
says, "Let's watch something else."

"But we have to watch the whole season to see
who wins."

"Ryan, you can watch it another time. There are other shows on Netflix, you know."

"Just one more. Please."

"Fine." Ray tosses the control on the sofa, gets up, and goes to Mom's room. Is he going to tell on me? I stand up and walk just a little closer so I can hear what he says.

"Mom, can I go ride bikes with Logan and Aiden?"

Mom yawns. "Um, yes. But only for an hour. I'm going to get dinner started soon."

Before Mom closes her door, I say, "Can I go, too?"

Ray yells, "No. No, you can't come! Mom, please—she can't come this time."

"Ray, stop being so mean," I say.

Mom comes out of her room. "Both of you quiet down. Your father is sleeping."

"But Mom, I just want to hang out with my friends. I don't want to worry about Ryan keeping up with me or if she's going to get attacked by bees."

"It's not my fault those bees chased after me! You just don't want me to come because I beat you racing and you're embarrassed that your little sister is faster than you."

"You're not faster than me. I had just raced Aiden and—"

"Quiet! Both of you," Mom yells, even though she's telling us to be quiet. "Ryan, let Ray go be with his friends today. Why don't you stay here and help me with dinner?" She walks into the kitchen and washes her hands. "One hour, Ray. Don't be a minute late."

Ray leaves and I go into the kitchen. Yes, I love to cook, but I don't think it's fair that Ray gets to go outside while I'm here. Mom takes the defrosted chicken wings out of the fridge, rinses them, and says, "You season and I'll flour and fry."

I nod.

The phone rings and Mom steps into the living room. She covers the phone with her hand and whispers to me, "Easy on the salt."

"Right. Easy on the salt," I say, and as soon as I say it, I get an idea for getting back at Ray for being rude and not wanting me to come with him. Easy on the salt but not on the pepper. Or the hot sauce. I double-check to make sure Mom is not looking and slide four wings to the side. I do the usual seasoning Mom always does and then I add triple the amount of pepper to the four wings set aside for Ray. I open the cabinet and get the hot sauce out that always makes Dad's eyes water. When I open the bottle, my nose tickles. I coat the four wings in the hot sauce—drenching them in the liquid fire. Then, before Mom

comes back, I rub them in flour so she won't see the sauce or extra, extra, extra pepper. I flour the other wings and keep them separate.

When Mom is off the phone, she pours oil in the iron skillet. I make sure she fries the regular wings first. They sizzle in the oil and once they are ready, she takes them out of the pan and rests them on a plate that's covered with a paper towel to soak up the extra oil. Then she's ready for the last four wings. The fire wings. They cook to a golden brown and when they are finished, I make sure to grab Ray's fire wings first. "This plate is for Ray," I say.

"Thanks, sweetheart. Go ahead and make yours and I'll make mine and your dad's." Mom plops a scoop of mashed potatoes onto her plate.

I sit down at the dining room table next to Ray.

Dad prays, "God, we thank you for this food. Please bless it and bless the hands that prepared it."

When Dad prays this, I get nervous and wonder if God will still bless me even though I've made Ray's food extra, extra, extra hot. I don't realize I'm staring at Ray's plate until Mom says, "Ryan, why aren't you eating?"

I pick up a spoonful of potatoes and eat.

Ray hasn't touched his chicken yet. He eats everything one at a time. All the corn, all the potatoes. Then he picks up a wing and before biting into it he says, "We had so much fun riding our bikes today. And no one got attacked by bees."

"Ray, don't start," Dad says.

And I don't even say anything because I know what's coming. That'll teach him to make fun of me.

Ray says, "I'm not starting. I'm just stating a fact. We had fun. No threat of bee stings . . ." And then he bites into his chicken. "Whoa!" Ray yelps and throws the half-eaten wing back on the plate. "Why is this chicken so hot?" He grabs his water and gulps it down. His eyes are watering and he starts coughing.

Mom puts her napkin in her lap. "Honey, you are exaggerating. This chicken is not spicy at all." She picks up a wing from his plate to taste it.

"Don't!" I shout. "Don't eat that."

"Ryan, what did you do?" She sets the chicken back on the plate.

Ray drinks more water. "Whatever she did is making my lips burn." He goes into the kitchen. I hear the water running and Ray is coughing and coughing.

Mom goes into the kitchen. Dad picks up a fire wing and takes a bite. He grabs his water and rubs his eyes. He's not as dramatic as Ray but still it's too much for him, and this is a big deal because Dad has won hot-wing-eating contests and swears he has a tongue of steel. He shakes his head but also has a smile on his face.

"Ryan, come in here right now and apologize," Mom says. She is helping Ray recover, giving him a glass of milk. "After your apology you can go to your room."

I walk over to Ray and say, "You were being mean to me and you wouldn't let me ride bikes with you today, so I—"

"That is not an apology," Mom says.

"Well, I'm just explaining why I did it. Ray is always—"

"Ryan!" Now Dad is in here. He stands next to Mom, the two of them waiting for me to make this right.

"Okay, okay. I'm sorry."

"For what?" Dad says.

"I'm sorry for making your chicken extra, extra, extra hot and for tricking you into eating it."

Ray doesn't even turn around to face me. He just keeps drinking his milk.

"Go to your room," Mom says. "And think about what you did."

I go into my room and I am sure Mom and Dad think I am in here crying or regretting that I pranked Ray. But no. I change into my pajamas, get in bed, pull the covers up, and think about how I made Ray's chicken wings extra, extra, extra hot. And I laugh, laugh, laugh myself to sleep.

WHAT BROTHERS DO

"**BE WHO WE NAMED** you to be," Dad says to Ray before we leave for school the next day. I am still not used to Dad going to sleep while everyone else is waking up and getting ready for the day. Just before he goes into his room he says, "You two are brother and sister. You take care of each other no matter what, you hear me?"

"Yes, sir," Ray says.

"Ryan, I'm talking to you, too."

"Yes, sir."

We leave for school and we are quiet most of the way. I am the one who speaks first. "I'm sorry about the hot sauce."

Ray shrugs. "It was kind of funny. You went a little overboard, though. My tongue still feels numb."

We meet KiKi at her house and keep walking to school. When we get to Vernon, Ray goes to his class-room. Me and KiKi go to ours. It's a normal day, a good day even, until Ms. Barnes says to me, "It's not that you can't cook for the talent show. It's just that you can't use a deep fryer here. Maybe you can make your elephant ears ahead of time and just do a demonstration for the judges."

Clearly Ms. Barnes has never had elephant ears. They have to be served hot, straight out of the deep fryer, so all that buttery, cinnamon goodness melts in the judges' mouths. "A demonstration without the actual hot elephant ears won't be the same," I tell her.

"Well, is there something else you can make? Something that doesn't require a stove or oven or deep fryer?"

"Cooking requires at least one of those."

"How about you make a nice fresh salad? You can

come up with something unique to add to impress the judges, can't you?"

A salad? I'll definitely lose if I make a salad.

I tell Ms. Barnes I'll think about it and then I leave to meet Ray so we can walk home. KiKi has a doctor's appointment after school, so she's being picked up by her mom. As soon as I see Ray, I tell him what Ms. Barnes said. "I don't know what else to do besides cook. I won't be able to participate in the talent show."

Ray helps me brainstorm another talent to share. "You know how to play the piano. Why don't you do that?"

"I only know how to play 'Hot Cross Buns' and 'Mary Had a Little Lamb.'"

"But you play them well," Ray says. And I know this is him trying to live up to his name, like Dad always tells him to. It's nice of him, but I know my talent is not playing the piano. Not yet. "What if you film yourself cooking at our house and then you can show the video on the big screen. No one's ever used

technology in their presentation. That's original."
Ray reaches out to hold my hand as we pass the
house with the barking dogs. He knows I'm afraid
of dogs—even dogs behind gates who can't get to me.

He keeps on thinking up ideas for what I can do in
the talent show. I don't want to talk about it anymore.
I just want to think about it and come up with something on my own. But Ray is persistent. When we get
home he insists on me trying out recipes that I could
do at school.

After we eat dinner, Mom turns the kitchen over
to us, only helping out when I call her. "Okay," Ray
says. "What's something you can make that's quick
and tasty and doesn't require an oven, stovetop, or
deep fryer—or grill?"

At first I can't think of anything that would
be good but then I remember that Amanda really
liked the smoothie I made for her. Ms. Barnes didn't
say anything about a blender. "I can make my
Blackberry-Lime Extravaganza." (Amanda's name
for it was the perfect name after all.)

Ray doesn't help but he does give suggestions.

"You should add a vegetable. Adults will like that and all the fourth graders will be impressed that it still tastes good."

"Spinach! I can add spinach." I learned that spinach is good for you and when it's in smoothies you can't even taste it. I make the smoothie—but the spinach makes the texture a little weird, so I dump it out and try again, only Mom comes in and fusses at me for wasting food. "But Mom—the whole point is to experiment and try things out."

"Well, make less next time. And keep an eye on the clock. It'll be bedtime soon."

I try again. Ray and I drink it all but it doesn't taste that great. Not enough honey. Plus, the spinach makes the color too green.

"It's not *that* bad," Ray says.

"It's not that good, either."

Ray laughs, then I laugh, too, and the two of us sip and giggle until we are at the end of our smoothies.

"I don't have any talent," I say. "I'm not good at anything."

"You're good at lots of things. It's just that the

things you're good at aren't so easy to put on a stage," Ray says. "You're good at helping and being nice to people, and sharing—even with me when I'm getting on your nerves." Ray slurps his drink, making the most obnoxious loud sound. I slurp mine, too. And without even meaning to we make a rhythm and once we realize that, we keep it going and have a whole song happening made from our straws slurping and tapping the glasses.

Mom calls out that it's time for bed, but we keep our song going a little longer. Ray stops slurping and starts freestyling while I keep the beat going. The last part of his rhyme is about me.

"Ryan's got talent that matters most, she don't boast . . . her talent is the best, better than the rest . . . Ryan Hart got heart, her cookin' is art . . . her talent can't be seen, she's nice, not mean. Ryan's got talent that matters most . . ."

QUESTIONS

PORTLAND HAS HAD ONE whole week without rain, which means the sky stays blue long into the evening. June's sun has brought out hundreds of people to the market. After Mom unloads the car at her booth, we drive around and around trying to find a parking space. We end up parking far and on our way to the market, we pass a man on the corner who is begging for change. "Or food," he says. "I could use something to eat."

Mom goes into her purse and pulls out two dollars. "It's all I can give," she says. "But you know, there's a shelter not too far from here. And around the corner, there's a place where they give out free meals—no questions asked."

The man says, "And every day they give us lukewarm soup and rock-hard bread. No, thank you." The man walks away, then calls back, "But thank you for this." He waves the dollar bills in his hands.

When we get to the market, Amanda and I help Mom set up and then we are free to roam. The crowd is so thick, Amanda and I have to hold hands so we don't lose each other as we walk to our favorite booths. Amanda insists on stopping by the art man to get our Moonstruck chocolate, but I just want to hurry to the Scarves & Things booth so I can ask the woman who works there about her grandmother and the hairpins, the seashells, postcard, handkerchief, and rose petals.

"Are you really going to tell her you live in her grandmother's old house?" Amanda asks. We've stopped holding hands so she can unwrap her candy. "I don't know if this is a good idea."

"I'm not going to tell her anything. I'm just going

to ask her questions," I say. "I just want to see if her family is connected to my family."

When we get to the booth there is a long line and it's hard to get under the tent to start shopping and looking around. I don't see the woman who was here before and I can't get to the table where I saw the hairpin. We push our way through the crowd and finally, I see her. I probably should have practiced what I was going to say but I didn't, so when she says to me, "How can I help you?" I blurt out, "Did your grandmother live on Twenty-Third and Alberta Street?"

Amanda looks shocked that this is the very first question I asked, but I don't know how to casually bring it up, so I thought I'd just go for it.

"Well, ah, no—not that I know of. And what makes you ask that?"

"I just, well . . . hi. My name is Ryan Hart. My mom works over at the Hart to Heart booth." I nudge Amanda, who is standing there like she really believes this woman is some kind of ghost.

"Hi, I'm, uh, my name is Amanda."

"Well, hello. My name is Laura."

I clear my throat. "I think I might have something that belongs to your grandmother." I take the hairpins out of my pocket and hold them out in my hand.

"Oh my." The woman takes my hand and brings it closer to her. "Why, isn't this something? You have something very precious," she says. "But no one in my family lived on Alberta Street."

When she says this, my whole heart squeezes into a fist. "Are you sure?"

"I'm sure."

"But these look just like the hairpin you had on display in your booth." I tell the woman the whole story—how I am living in a new (old) house, how I found the tin canister, how the hairpins match hers.

"Well, you know, these were very popular in the 1940s. They're what we call vintage. And so many women wore them. I'm sorry I don't know who these belonged to. But I am sure they are in good hands with you."

A customer comes over to ask the woman a question. I say goodbye and head back with Amanda to Mom's station. "Are you okay?" Amanda asks.

I shrug. "I guess." I try to act like it doesn't matter. But it does. I really want to know who lived in our house. I wanted to go home and tell Ray I figured out the mystery. But instead I walk with Amanda and we get to talking about the talent show and how I am not going to participate because I have no talent.

"You do too have talent! Don't say things like that," Amanda tells me.

"Well, yeah, I do. But not the kind that is good on a stage," I say. Ever since Ray said it, I believe it even more.

"But I thought all fourth graders have to participate."

"We do."

"So what are you going to do?"

"Well, participate doesn't mean perform onstage. KiKi is the MC and so that got me thinking about how there must be a lot of other roles Ms. Barnes needs," I say. "I'm going to ask Ms. Barnes if I can be an usher. Usually teachers seat their classes, but I can ask if I can greet everyone at the door and pass out the programs. That should count, right?"

"Yep."

"And being friendly isn't necessarily a talent, but it is something I'm good at."

"True. There are definitely people who are mean and never smile that should never, ever be greeters."

And just like that I know what I can do for the talent show. I can even help prepare the programs. I'm sure Ms. Barnes will need help with that.

Amanda and I get back to Mom's booth. She has sold so many things today, we don't have a lot to pack up. Mom drops Amanda off and the moment we get home, Ray is asking me all kinds of questions about the woman and the hairpin. "Did you see the woman? Did you find out who it belongs to?"

So many questions.

"No," I answer.

Ray doesn't say *I told you so* or anything mean to

rub it in my face. I think maybe he wants to know just as much as I do. "Maybe it's good we don't know. Maybe it's some sad story and you should just put it back in your closet. Or throw it out in the garbage."

"Maybe," I say, even though I am absolutely not throwing any of it away.

I go to bed tonight thinking about how I'll go to school on Monday and ask Ms. Barnes if I can be a greeter for the talent show, then I start thinking again about the tin canister and who it belonged to. I wonder, what if Ray and Amanda have it wrong? What if the woman who lived here left it all behind on purpose? Maybe it's some kind of welcome gift— some kind of special tin that I should keep and add on to and leave behind for the next person who sleeps in this room.

19

WAYS TO MAKE SUNSHINE

"YOU THINK THEY'LL CANCEL the parade?" Amanda asks.

"Commercials said rain or shine," I tell her.

Amanda and Zoe are at my house because Mom and Dad are taking us to the Grand Floral Parade. It's Rose Festival Month and there are all kinds of celebrations happening. Every year we go to the parade, bringing our folding chairs and reserving our spot where everything kicks off, at the Memorial Coliseum. We pack peanut butter and jelly sandwiches and fruit and chips and water and Dad brings his binoculars so we see every detail of the floats up close. Every single year my voice gets hoarse because I yell and cheer so loud.

But this year, I don't think we're going.

It is raining. Well, it's not raining—it's storming, actually. And none of us want to sit under a crying sky.

I go into the kitchen, where Mom is unpacking our picnic basket, and say, "But Mom, can't we buy tickets to sit inside at the coliseum where the parade begins?"

Ray blurts out, "We don't have money for that, Ryan. You know that."

"Besides," Mom says, "they're probably all sold out."

"Well, what are we going to do?"

Ray walks out of the kitchen saying, "I'm going to play video games with Dad."

I look at Mom and she doesn't even let me get another word out. "Ryan, there's plenty to do here at the house. Use your imagination."

"But we wanted to go to the parade."

"I did, too, sweetheart. But that's not what's happening today. We'll still get to do something for Rose Festival. We'll go to the city fair next weekend."

"But Mom—"

"Ryan, what do you want me to do? I can't control the weather. You've got company—go play with them. The three of you should be able to come up with something." She unpacks the last of the lunch and says, "Let me know when you're ready to eat." Mom walks into the living room and grabs her knitting needles.

I stand in the kitchen looking at the wicker basket Mom had taken out, the blankets and chairs we were going to bring that are already at the back door, ready to be loaded into the car. I pick up one of the chairs and the blanket and take them to my room. I pass Mom on the way; she doesn't even look up from her yarn.

When I get to my room, I say to Amanda, "If we can't go to the parade, let's have one here." I set the chair up against the wall. "Come on, help me with the other stuff. Zoe, you stay here and get the audience ready." I point to my bin of teddy bears and Barbie dolls. "Set them up in the chair and along the rest of the wall, okay?"

"Okay!" Zoe says. She jumps off my bed and gets to work.

Amanda and I go back into the kitchen. We get the other chairs and the food Mom put away. I stuff it in the basket—not as neat as she would, but I get it to fit. We walk back to my room, passing Mom again. This time she looks up. "What are you girls doing?"

"Using our imaginations like you told us to," I say.

Mom gives me a serious look. "I don't want you making a mess in there."

"I won't. I promise."

When we get back to my room Zoe has set all the bears and dolls against the wall. "What else?" she asks.

"Well, next we need to make some sunshine."

Zoe looks confused and Amanda says, "How are we going to do that?"

I go to my desk and take out the pack of construction paper I have. It has every color of the rainbow over and over in a pattern: red, orange, yellow, green, blue, indigo, violet, red, orange, yellow, green, blue, indigo, violet.

I pull out all the yellow paper, then grab scissors and three pencils. "Let's make suns and we'll cut them out and tape them all over my room."

Zoe spreads out on the floor and gets to drawing. Her circles aren't that great but I like that she puts a smiley face and big brown eyes on every sun she makes. Amanda says, "Zoe, I'll cut them for you, okay?"

We make all different shapes and sizes of suns and I tape them on the wall, on the window, on my closet door. We make clouds, too—big and white like the fluffy ones that should be in the sky on a day when there's a parade.

"It's still not that bright, though," Amanda says.

We think and think and think and then I shout, "I know!" I go to the lamp on my desk and turn it on. It's the kind that twists and turns all kinds of ways, so I

bend the lamp, turning the light up so it shines toward the ceiling.

"Wow, it's so much brighter. Do you have another one?"

"No, but Ray does in his room."

We probably should ask first, but Ray is at the arcade with Dad, so I just tiptoe to his room, walk over to his desk, unplug his lamp, and run back to my room. Once we have Ray's light on and the blinds pulled all the way up so the natural light can come in, the room looks bright. We lay out the blanket and unpack the picnic basket and everything is ready.

"But who's going to be in the parade?" Zoe asks.

I smile. "We are."

"Yeah, we can each take turns," Amanda says.

"And we can use Ray's scooter so we have something to ride on. We can pretend it's the float." He doesn't even ride it anymore. I don't know why he still has it.

This means I have to go back to Ray's room. This time I must not tiptoe soft enough, because Mom calls out, "Ryan, what are you doing in Ray's room?"

"Nothing!"

"Ryan?"

"I'm not doing anything. I just needed to get something." I pull the scooter to my room and close my door.

"Ryan, you should go first," Amanda says. "You can be one of the Rose Festival Princesses."

That was the whole reason why we wanted to go to the parade. We wanted to see the Rose Festival Court. Fourteen girls, one from each Portland public high school, are chosen to be princesses. They get to do all kinds of amazing things like meet the mayor and talk about things that matter to them. They get to travel by tour bus and take a trip to Pendleton and ride horses.

The two best things are that they get to have a whole new wardrobe—and all of them dress alike everywhere they go—plus they get to be in the Grand Floral Parade. All fourteen of them waving from the float that snails by with most of Portland camped out on sidewalks just to see them. I wanted to wave at the princess from Jefferson High School. That's the high school I'll be going to one day. Mom's brother and sister and even her mom and dad went there, so me and Ray are going, too. Maybe I'll be a princess one day and I'll get to tell the mayor how we should start a program that feeds the hungry. How we should cook gourmet meals for them, food that's healthy and so good, everyone will want to eat it. Not just starving people. Because everyone deserves to have something in their bellies other than not-that-hot soup and rock-hard bread.

"Okay, well, I have to go get dressed," I tell Amanda. I go into the closet and pull out the dress I wore on Easter plus the tin and take one of the hairpins out. I pull my hair up and try to get it to look fancy. Once I am all ready, Amanda plays music from her iPad. We blast it as loud as I think Mom will allow and I put one foot on Ray's scooter and ride around my room slowly, waving like the girls who ride the floats do, elbow bent, wrist stiff and turning side to side.

Amanda and Zoe cheer. I go around the room

twice. It's kind of hard because the bed is in the way, so I can't do a complete circle, but still it's fun and it makes me wonder how it must feel in real life. When I get back to where I started, Amanda says, "My turn, my turn!" and she transforms herself into a girl who dances ahead of the marching band. "I'm a drum major," she says. She uses my ruler as her baton. I give her my whistle, the one from one of those vending machines that have the big silver claw that picks up a prize (or what Dad calls "more junk"). Amanda blows and blows and lifts her knees up high and when one of her favorite songs comes on she starts dancing for real—not pretend—and Zoe starts dancing, too, so I join them and we are laughing and singing to the music. When the song is over Zoe says, "Look, it's not raining anymore! Look what we did!"

She thinks we made the rain stop. At first I start to explain that we didn't but instead of disagreeing with her, I just sing along to the next song and keep dancing.

Practice Makes Perfect

WE'VE BEEN COUNTING DOWN to the last day of school. Once the dismissal bell rings today, there's only one more day to count. Tomorrow is the last day. Tomorrow is also the talent show. I am in the multi-purpose room during lunch folding programs and listening to KiKi as she rehearses the script. "Ms. Barnes said I don't have to memorize it but I should familiarize myself with it so I don't have to keep my eyes glued to the paper. She wants me to be able to look up and make eye contact with the audience," KiKi tells me.

I fold and fold while KiKi practices the opening welcome.

I fold and fold while KiKi pronounces names she is not familiar with over and over.

I fold and fold while KiKi proclaims the winner. For now, she is just testing out how excited she should be. She changes her voice three different times, saying, "And the judges have made their decision. Our fourth-grade talent show first place goes to . . . Ryan Hart!"

My name is just a placeholder for now, of course, but it feels good to hear it booming over the microphone. KiKi says, "Okay. One more time and then I'll be ready to go."

"Okay."

KiKi begins. "Welcome to our annual Fourth-Grade Talent Showcase . . ."

Just then, Hannah walks in.

"Hi," Hannah says. "Ms. Barnes said I could practice in here once you are finished."

"We're going to be a while," KiKi says.

I clear my throat and give KiKi a look. I am trying to live up to this name that means "leader." "But you can stay," I say. "We can take turns practicing."

"Thanks," Hannah says. She drops her book bag on the floor and sits next to me. "Need help?" She picks up one of the photocopied programs and folds.

KiKi rolls her eyes but continues practicing her introductions. Then she says, "And now, please welcome Hannah Wilkerson to the stage."

Hannah gets up and performs her song and I can't even keep folding or do anything else. All I can do is watch her stand in the middle of the stage and sing. When she is finished, I stand and cheer and whistle and even KiKi gives in to a little clap (but she doesn't stand).

"Hannah, you sound so good," I say.

"Thank you. I am so nervous," she tells us.

"You are?" I sit back down and start folding. She joins me and KiKi does, too.

"Yeah, I love to sing but every single time, I get butterflies in my stomach. They flutter and make me feel like when I open my mouth nothing will come out."

"I never thought that even people with a whole lot of talent get nervous, too," I say.

"Ms. Barnes says being nervous means you care about what you're going to do. It's okay to be nervous, you just have to use those nerves as energy to do your best," Hannah tells us.

We are done folding all the programs.

KiKi says, "Hannah, you want to practice one more time?"

Hannah sings and, again, we cheer her on. This time KiKi might be louder than me. "She's actually really good," KiKi says.

"Yeah, she is," I say. "You're good at what you do, too. We all are."

BELIEVING

ONCE RAY AND I get home, we change out of our school clothes and are free to do whatever we want. The best part of the day before the last day of school is there is no homework. The other good thing is that I get to plan out my Last Day of School Tradition with Mom. Tomorrow, the plan is that Mom will pick us up from school and we'll go to the North Portland Library. Like every other last day of school, I'll get to pick out one cookbook and one chapter book. Then Mom and I will sit at one of the tables, and she'll pull out her special three-month calendar and we'll plan our summer. Always, we include a trip to Oaks

Amusement Park, an afternoon at OMSI, a trip to Seaside Beach, and more walks to the library. Mom lets me invite Amanda and KiKi to some of the outings and we always plan a cookout on the Fourth of July.

This summer is going to be the best ever. I'll be able to go over to Amanda's and get in the pool—this time fully prepared. And she'll be able to spend the night. Maybe we can have sleepovers with KiKi joining us, too.

Just one more day and summer will be here and I can start making all the plans with Mom.

I am in the kitchen helping Mom prepare a snack. We're making peanut butter and jelly skewers. I am spreading the peanut butter and jelly and Mom is cutting the sandwiches in fours. Then we take thick, wooden sticks and push one sandwich square on, adding half a strawberry on the stick, and then another sandwich square and another strawberry until the stick is full and we move on to the next one.

"All that work for a PB and J sandwich?" Ray asks.

"You'll like it once you eat it," I tell him.

"Of course I will, but why go through all that trouble when I'm just going to pull it off and eat it anyway?" He reaches for a sandwich square as if he's going to eat it.

The doorbell rings, so Ray leaves me alone and goes into the living room.

Mom calls out, "Ask who it is before answering!"

I hear Ray ask who it is and a woman says, "Laura Adams . . . Is this the home of Tamia Hart?"

As soon as I hear the voice I know it's Ms. Laura from Saturday Market. Mom and I go into the living room. "Hello, Tamia. I'm sorry to barge in like this but I just had to stop by."

"Oh, no, please don't apologize. Come on in."

"I'm actually here to talk with your daughter."

"Me?" I say.

"Ryan?" Mom asks.

Mom offers her a seat on the sofa and gives Ray a look that tells him to turn the television off. Ms. Laura says to me, "I haven't been able to get you out of my mind ever since you came by to ask about the hairpin."

When she says this, Mom gives me a look like I've got a lot of explaining to do once Ms. Laura leaves.

"Well, like I said, none of my family have ever lived here but I asked my mother if maybe she knew who did." Ms. Laura hands me a black-and-white photo. There are two young girls in the picture— one Black, one white. They are wearing the kind of dresses Mom makes me wear on Easter and standing under a sign that says Portland's Junior Rose Festival court. And in their hair? They each have a hairpin that looks just like the ones upstairs in the canister, just like the one at the market.

"Do you know the girl your grandma is with?" I ask.

"I don't. But on the back, it has her name and the year 1945."

She turns the photo over and I see the names Mary Beth and Gloria Mae.

Gloria Mae. The Black girl's name is Gloria.

Ms. Laura keeps talking, "Honestly, I'm not sure if Gloria lived here or if these hairpins were hers or my grandmother's, but when I saw this photo, I just had to show you."

I stare at the photo, try to memorize every part of it. I think back to playtime with Amanda and Zoe and I ask, "So they were Rose Festival Princesses?"

"Well, no. I don't think so. Looks like maybe they were at a dance for teens or some kind of community celebration to honor the Rose Festival Court," Ms. Laura says. She points to the people in the background who are standing around, some dancing, some eating. "Looks like a grand celebration."

Mom says, "Wow, what a coincidence." And I know this means she doesn't think the little girl in that photo lived here. But I believe.

I believe Mary Beth's hair kept falling in her face and getting in the way—like hair does sometimes—and she asked her friend Gloria if she could borrow a hairpin. I believe they danced all night at the neighborhood celebration. And maybe they even waved to the girls on the floats the next day at the parade. Maybe they stood in the same place we usually stand, right at the beginning where everything kicks off.

Maybe, the other day, Amanda, Zoe, and I really did make the sun shine.

22

The Show Must Go On

Just as Ray and I leave to walk to school, the phone rings. Mom answers it and when she hangs up she says, "You two don't have to stop by KiKi's along the way. She's sick today, so she won't be going to school."

"But today's the talent show. She's the MC," I say.

"Well, they'll have to find someone else." Mom walks over to the door and kisses me on my forehead. "I'll be picking you two up after school, okay?"

"Okay," we say.

When we pass KiKi's house, I almost go knock on her door to double-check that she is really sick. I mean, there's sick-sick and there's

I-don't-feel-that-great sick. If she just doesn't feel that great, she should come to school. She's practiced and practiced. Who will MC the show now?

Once we get to school, the day is pretty much like every other day, except at the end of lunch, I get to go to the multipurpose room to prepare for the talent show. All students who are setting up, working backstage, or performing are dismissed early.

When I get to the auditorium, I find Ms. Barnes pacing back and forth. I overhear our librarian, who is the stage manager, saying to her, "Sorry to be the bearer of bad news, but one of our judges just called and canceled."

"What else can go wrong?" Ms. Barnes says. "We're down a judge and our MC is out." She shakes her head. "Well, 'the show must go on' just took on a very real meaning."

I walk over to the stage. "Ms. Barnes," I say. "I—I think I can help. I'm familiar with the script because I helped KiKi practice, so, I . . . I think I can be the MC if you need someone to take her place."

I can do this. I can live up to my name.

"Well, Ryan Hart, that's just—that would be amazing." She hugs me and says, "Come with me." We go to the front of the room and stand at the podium. As soon as we get to the podium and I look out at the whole room, the whole wide room that can fit hundreds of people, I realize what I've just done.

I take a deep breath.

I can do this.

I just have to try.

Ms. Barnes hands me a folder that has the script typed out in a big font. "Take some time to practice," she says. Ms. Barnes gives me all kinds of instructions but I can't really hear her over my pounding heart.

I start reading the script and remembering the many times I heard KiKi say these lines.

I take a deep breath.

I can do this.

I just have to try.

Soon, the fourth graders arrive and we test the mic and meet the judges and now it's time. First, second, and third graders fill the room, the youngest students up front. I am peeking out of the curtain and taking deep, deep breaths when I feel a hand on my shoulder. I turn around. It's Hannah.

"I can't do this," she says.

"What? Yes you can. You can do this. We can do this."

Hannah doesn't look like she believes me.

"You told me nerves are good, right? That we can use that energy to push us to do our best—all we can do is our best."

"Wait, *our*? I thought you were—"

"KiKi is sick."

"Whoa. And you're going to take her place?"

"See? If I can go out there and talk in front of all those people, you can go out there and sing in front of all those people."

Hannah closes her eyes, breathes in, out. "Okay. We can do this."

Ms. Barnes comes backstage and says, "Ready? It's time."

She brings me out on the stage. She is holding my hand and I am so glad because if she weren't I might just run away. As soon as we walk onto the stage, the audience starts clapping and I hear someone yelling my name. I follow the voice. It's Dad standing next to Ray in the way back of the room. Ms. Barnes whispers to me, "I thought you could use some encouragement."

Dad is here, even though he should be sleeping now. Dad is here and he already looks proud of me even though I haven't even opened my mouth.

Ms. Barnes lets go of my hand and adjusts the microphone for me.

I step up to the podium. "Good afternoon, Vernon!" When I say this, everyone cheers again and I know my voice can be heard with no issues of the sound being too low or too high. My nerves settle, just a tiny bit, and for this first part, I don't even need to look at the script. "Welcome to our annual Fourth-Grade Talent Showcase."

ANOTHER THING ABOUT ICE CREAM

MOM PICKS US UP after school and we go to Helen Bernhard Bakery on Broadway to pick up a cake. The whole way there Dad and Ray tell Mom how good I was, how I didn't mess up, not once. "I am so proud of you, Ryan. I am really, really proud," Mom says.

After we get the cake we stop at Safeway and get ice cream. I think maybe Mom is celebrating how well I did, how much I am growing into my name. But when we get home, I realize this cake and ice cream celebration has nothing to do with me stepping in for KiKi. And just when I thought my favorite dessert couldn't be ruined any more, I learn that Mom and Dad have many, many ways of messing up a good day, and a favorite treat.

Mom uncovers a cake that looks like it's been painted with pink icing. The cake is decorated with the prettiest white roses. In the middle there's a math equation in white icing: $2 + 1 = 3$. I read it out loud twice before I understand what's happening. The pink icing, the number three, the way Mom is holding her belly. Dad says, "Our family is growing."

And Mom adds, "You two are getting a little sister." Her whole face is a shining sun.

Ray says, "Another one? Really? Why can't it be a brother?"

"Because God blessed us with another girl," Dad says. He cuts the cake and dishes out ice cream.

The only thing worse than having ice cream when learning that you are moving is having it when you learn that you are going to be a big sister.

Ray shrugs and starts eating his dessert.

There will be five of us in this new (old) house that I am just starting to get comfortable in.

This is not something to celebrate.

Not only is this little baby ruining ice cream and cake. She's doing it on the last day of school, on the day that I grew into my name and pushed through my fear to speak in front of my classmates (plus all the special guests). All day long I've been so excited to start summer vacation. All day long I've been thinking how I am no longer a fourth grader. But Mom hasn't even mentioned that I am officially in the fifth grade. She hasn't said anything about our Last Day of School Tradition of going to the public library.

What if Mom will be too tired or too busy getting ready for the baby this summer? Will I get to do anything we normally do? Mom hasn't said anything about going to Oaks Amusement Park, or when we'll go to Seaside Beach, or what we'll do for the Fourth of July. All she is talking about is baby this and baby that.

Ray doesn't seem bothered at all by this baby news. Between mouthfuls of cake and ice cream, he says, "Mom, there's *really* a baby growing inside of you?" He stares at Mom's belly.

"Yes, there is." Mom rubs her stomach, stands, and turns to the side pinching her shirt tight to her body. Her stomach is poking out, just a little. "She's right here," Mom says. "Soon you'll be able to notice without having to look too hard." Mom sits back down and eats a bite of her cake. "Ray, do you remember when I was pregnant with Ryan?"

Ray shrugs and says, "Not really." He licks the frosting off his fork.

This just proves to me that this baby is nothing but trouble. She's going to be remembered and I'm not? *Hmph.* I shrug my shoulders just like he did and tell him, "Well, I don't remember you growing in Mom's belly, either, so there."

"How could you? I'm older, *duuuh!*" The way he says *duh*, dragging it out like an accordion, makes me even more upset. Ray gets up and puts his plate in the sink.

When Ray comes back to the table, Dad cuts another slice of cake for himself. "Do either of you have any questions for us?" he asks.

Ray asks a very important question. One I hadn't thought of. "Where's the baby going to sleep?"

"Well," Dad says, "the baby will sleep in a crib that will be in our room for the first few months." He gets up from the table, walks over to the refrigerator, and pours himself a glass of milk.

Mom adds, "Once she's old enough to sleep in her own bed, she'll share the room with Ryan."

Me?

So far this little sister that everyone is so happy about has ruined my favorite dessert and will take over my bedroom. There is definitely nothing to celebrate here. I ask, "Where will she sit in the car?"

Mom looks puzzled, like she hasn't thought about it yet, and then she says, "In the back with you and Ray. We'll put her car seat on the passenger's side. You will sit in the middle and Ray will sit next to you."

"I won't be able to look out of the window

anymore?" I ask. Once the baby is here, I'll be smushed between my big brother and my little sister because two plus one equals three, and that puts me in the middle. How will I see the license plates as we drive through the city? Maybe this little baby sister is here to make Mom forget about *all* the things that are important to me.

Dad nudges me, says, "Ryan, you haven't eaten any of your cake."

Mom looks at me with care in her eyes and reaches out for my hand. "Sweetheart, things will change but you know what will never ever change?"

"What?" I ask.

"Our love for you."

I think about the story my little sister will be told about the day her big sister found out about her being in her momma's belly. I don't want her to know I refused to eat the cake and ice cream, that I complained about all the things that wouldn't be the same. I think to myself how awful that would feel to know her big sister was so upset. That would be worse than a sibling saying they didn't remember you being born.

Ray and Dad leave the table.

Mom stays with me. She slides my plate in the middle of the two of us. The ice cream runs rivers around the cake. She cuts the cake in half, slides my fork closer to me, and we start eating. The cake tastes so good, like all chocolate cake does, and so I'm glad I didn't waste it. I eat the last bite, set my fork on the plate.

I wonder if my little sister will like chocolate cake and chocolate ice cream. I wonder if she'll have adventurous taste buds and if she'll like playing chef with me and be taste tester for all the concoctions I cook up. Will she like having make-believe parades? Will she know how to make the sun shine even on the rainiest of days?

I wonder what we will call her and how long it will take her to grow into her name. I wonder if when we take a family vote, she'll side with me and Mom.

I do more math equations in my head:

$2 + 1 = 3$.

1 brother + 2 sisters = more girls.

1 dad + 1 brother + 1 mom + 2 sisters = more girls.

I am starting to think that the equation written in icing was good news after all.

I say to Mom, "There will be three girls in the house now."

"Yes, there will be," she says. She takes our dishes

to the sink. "Us girls outnumber the boys." She winks at me and smiles.

I think maybe things will get better and better from here.

ACKNOWLEDGMENTS

The best part of writing this novel was the remembering, the going back to the places in Portland that raised me: Vernon Elementary School, Alberta Park, Antioch Missionary Baptist Church. So many of these tales were inspired by real memories from my childhood as well the experiences I've shared in helping to raise my nieces, nephews, and goddaughter. Sydney, Tobias, Caleb, Nehemiah, and Ryan, I love watching you grow and learn and soar. You bring such light into my life.

Thank you to Kori Johnson and Ellen Hagan for being early readers and for your invaluable feedback during the writing process. And, always, thank you to my agent, Rosemary Stimola, and my editor, Sarah Shumway.